Once Upon an Adventure

J. E. Mueller

ONCE UPON AN ADVENTURE

J.E. MUELLER

CONTENTS

PROLOGUE 1
CHAPTER 1 3
CHAPTER 2 18
CHAPTER 3 33
CHAPTER 4 45
CHAPTER 5 57
CHAPTER 6 70
CHAPTER 7 82
CHAPTER 8 99
CHAPTER 9 109
EPILOGUE 138
BONUS SCENE 141
CHARACTER PROFILES 144
TIMELINE 149
ACKNOWLEDGMENTS 150
ABOUT THE AUTHOR 151
ALSO BY J.E. MUELLER 152

*To all of those who wanted a little more magic,
And another happily ever after, again.
Also to Nico, Geetha, and Aud.
Words cannot express how much I adore you.*

PROLOGUE

A fierce wind swept around the clearing like a winter gale. Branches held tight onto the trees, while leaves slowly gave into the gust and blew in a circle. After a few moments, everything came to a standstill revealing two figures alone in a clearing just as the sun began to set.

"I've heard your intriguing call. Tell me, what exactly is it that you seek?" a cold female voice asked as she crossed her arms.

Donny assessed the cloaked woman. Her face was barely visible except for a rather unsettling, sinister smile. The dark red of her lips almost looked bloodstained, and they already stood out too vibrantly against her fair skin. He ignored those facts as best he could. Mustering all the courage he had, he let his anger take hold of his demands. "I want revenge on that idiot who locked me up, and for my Belle to see I am the best, most desirable, and most handsome in the land."

The woman gave a low chuckle. "To be the fairest one of all, you must complete a task for me, then I'll see that your competition is removed for a while. I will give you a charm to lend you aid, but if you fail from there, nothing more can be done."

"I'll do your task," Donny agreed without another thought. "Say the word and it will be done." He nodded his head vigorously, eager to begin and get what he wanted.

"I had a feeling you'd agree." She held out a slip of paper, seemingly coming from nowhere, and handed it over to him.

Donny couldn't tell with the darkening sky if it was magic or sleight of hand. Not that it mattered. Carefully, he unfolded the paper and scoffed as he read the words. "Impossible!"

"Oh, nothing is impossible, young simpleton." An amused smile crossed her face. "There are those determined to achieve their goals and those who are afraid of a little challenge."

"I'm not afraid!" Donny shot back, the insult quickly solidifying his resolve. "I just don't know where to find unicorns or werewolf fur. Swan feathers take nothing."

"The quest is to find, the challenge is to succeed. Do you accept?" Her sinister smile never faltered.

"I do." Donny replied through clenched teeth. While unable to turn down the challenge and its rewards, he knew he was in over his head.

"Perfect. Call for me when you've completed the tasks." A gale once more tore through the clearing, causing Donny to shield his eyes.

Once the wind died down, the woman was gone.

CHAPTER ONE

----Arnessa----

"As the group slowly descends the darkening stairs, you hear creaking from somewhere below you..." Nadia flashed a sinister smile from behind her dungeon master screen.

"I put my hand out to stop the group and roll to check for traps," Rey declared, tossing his dice into the center of the long table we sat at. We watched it land on fifteen. "With my modifier that's eighteen."

It had been a year since we started gaming together. We tried to meet at least once a month in person for some sort of adventure. Occasionally we'd meet online, when time and duties weren't always in our favor. Still, it was exciting to do something so wonderfully simple as game.

We glanced from Rey's smug smile over at Nadia who checked her sheet before smiling. "You notice that a step two down from you looks off. It seems to be raised more than the others."

Rey nodded and went back to talking in character. "There's a faulty step ahead. I'm not sure what it'll do."

"Trigger it!" I declared while grabbing a handful of chips. We had all sorts of junk food spread out for tonight's meetup, thanks mostly to everyone being tired of fancy meals and obligations. "If it spits something out, we'll know what the traps are on the rest of the steps, if there are any." I quickly ate the chips while Rey shook his head at me.

Vincent gave me a sidelong look. "I don't think that's wise Arnessa -er um." He glanced at my character sheet for the name. "Lydia. It could trap us here instead."

Ash shook her head. "No, I say we do it. It wouldn't trap us in the stairwell. We'd either have to find a new way down or find our way out by continuing through. Let's do it!"

"I am not stepping on it." Rey leaned back in his chair.

Cat snickered. "I remove a goblet from my pack and carefully toss it on the step."

"Roll for it." Nadia's lips twitched up into an almost menacing look.

Cat cursed under her breath as she cast her dice. Two.

"It bounces off the edge and doesn't trigger anything. You hear it clank and clatter down several more steps into the darkness. As it stops you hear something slam into a solid object. From where you are, you cannot tell if it's the door or the wall." Nadia glanced up at her expectantly.

"Let me try." I nodded over toward Cat.

"Use your own loot." Cat stuck her tongue out at me.

"Dirty rogue." I threw back at her. My wizard hadn't exactly been getting along with her for most, if any, of the trip. "I use my staff to reach out and press down on the step."

Nadia gave us a gleeful smile. "You hear the sound of metal hitting stone behind you."

"The entrance is blocked isn't it?" Rey sighed knowingly.

"I'll go back up the steps and check." Vincent glanced at Nadia for confirmation.

"At the top you see a barred gate is now down." Nadia's glee turned into an evil smirk.

"Is there a way out, or a switch nearby?" Vincent asked hopefully, shifting all of our attention back to our too cheerful DM.

"Roll for perception." Nadia replied in a sing-song voice.

Vincent groaned and rolled his dice. "Natural twenty! Yes!" He fist-pumped the air.

All eyes were on Nadia again. Would we be forced down to investigate the creepy loud sound? Would we be allowed to retreat if needed? The anticipation was invigorating, and exactly why I dragged Vincent to this monthly meet-up.

"You don't see a switch on this side, but through the bars, well out of reach looks like something that could be one. As you peer through, you see what looks like dried blood on the iron bars."

Vincent nodded. "I head back down and tell them what I found."

"At least it wasn't poison arrows." Cat shrugged, not bothered by the predicament. We had run into that a few sessions ago and nearly lost half the party.

"And the stairs didn't turn into a sudden slide," Ash let out a gleeful cheer. "Down we go!"

"I follow behind her, giving a step in between us." Rey stated.

"Same." the rest of us echoed with a laugh.

"Cowards." Ash chuckled, not even trying to amend her actions.

"As you descend the stairs, the darkness increases." Nadia said in a mysterious tone.

"I grab a torch from further up." I declared, not wanting to be caught too off guard, even with Ash as bait.

Nadia gave a nod. "With the added glow of light, you make it to the bottom. You see a steel door with bloodied handprints on it.

I liked to imagine our group staring at each other unsure how to proceed. In reality, Rey was eating his fifth slice of pizza staring off into space while he thought of what to do next.

"Who has the best lock check?" Vincent asked in between bites of pizza. I hadn't even seen him take another slice.

"I should." Cat sighed. "But my rolls have been terrible."

"Well, we can always try opening it first," Ash suggested. "But we should probably wait. Whatever was making that noise is likely on the other side of the door, and we'd want it to lose interest in the area, if at all possible."

"True. That would be smart, assuming it's not a small hall or passageway. Then we could sneak up on it." Rey agreed as he stacked his different dice into a tower.

"Let's try the door and be ready for a fight," Vincent said thoughtfully. "If it's unlocked, we're ready to go. If it is locked, we can get that figured out *and then* wait since we'd likely be making noise during that process."

Nadia smirked at us, a bit too cheerfully as we debated the better route to take here. "Decisions, decisions. What ever shall it be?" she taunted us.

Ash raised an eyebrow at her. "Stop that!" I laughed at how easily Nadia could rile her up.

"Ugh, I give. Let's vote," Rey called over the light noise our discussion was making. "Hands up, who says we try to open it first."

Everyone but Cat and Ash raised their hands.

"Let's do it!" Vincent called dramatically. "I hold my weapon at the ready as I carefully try to open the door with my non-dominant hand."

Nadia looked pleased. "You open the door and a body falls into the room. It's a bloodied mess. From the claw marks along its neck, you can see that he is dead. Past the body, a fresh trail of blood goes off into the darkness."

"What does the area look like?" I asked, hoping for some sort of clue to the situation we were in.

"There is a single torch on the other side of the door. A double wide stone corridor is all you can make out from the lack of sufficient light." Nadia seemed too pleased with herself in this dark adventure.

Cat groaned, rubbing her hands down her face. "This is where the party finally dies isn't it?"

"Come on, have some hope. We did survive the last campaign." Rey chuckled, not sounding anymore convinced than Cat was about the quest at hand.

"But not the two before that." Ash pointed out unhelpfully.

"But the first one we did survive as well." I commented before turning to Nadia. "How far into the hall can we see?"

"Not very. The torch gives you limited distance, but you can tell there is a light ahead." Nadia repeated for us. I had hoped for an additional hint or commentary but she wasn't budging.

"If we *carefully* move forward, we might be able to stealth through," Cat mused as she hummed to herself. "Someone should take the extra torch as well."

"Not with my armor. It's near impossible to move quietly and carefully," Rey sighed before glancing slowly around as he considered the scene. "This corpse either ran and hit the door before dying or was thrown over here after the goblet fell."

"What if it hit the door and died after locking the creature up?" I mused back, enjoying the theory.

"He would have slumped over." Ash shook her head. "This feels more staged."

"Should we just make enough noise to call the beast over and use the stairs and door to our current advantage?" Vincent asked.

"Let's do that!" Cat cheered, excited by the plan. "I retrieve the goblet that fell down here and throw it with all my might."

"Ugh." Rey and Ash groaned. At least this wasn't the worst impromptu decision anyone had made to date.

"I hastily take several steps back so I'm up a few stairs." I declared, wanting to be away from the door where I'd be able to use my spells better.

Nadia laughed before clearing her throat. "The goblet clangs off through the stone hall into the darkness, echoing with every bound before it settles. You hear something far off that sounds like it may be a scream cut short before silence blankets the hall once more."

"That was somehow worse than I was expecting." I grumble. Whatever was in there wasn't approaching us, yet. It did however have several things to kill. Or used to.

"I slowly lead the way into the darkness." Vincent said, making it sound more like a deathmarch than a winnable quest.

"I follow right behind." Rey declared, eagerness in his voice.

"Same," Cat agreed, equally determined. "Ash, grab the torch."

Ash glanced my way. "Well? Shall we?"

"Three steps behind, but better late than never." I agreed, curious to see where this story would take us.

Nadia grinned widely. "Good. Now roll for stealth."

Several dice hit the table just as the power went out.

Cold air draped around me like a blanket. It made no sense how it came out of nowhere just as the power went out. Magical lights didn't just randomly die like that. Carefully, I felt out for an illusion and was surprised that while I felt magic, there was no illusion there. Instead, just raw power met me. A shiver unrelated to the cold went down my spine and I was almost glad no one could see it.

"Um, Ash, can you dispel raw magic?" I asked softly, careful not to speak louder than necessary. I wasn't sure exactly how her magic worked, just that she had a terrible hold on it most days.

At first there was no reply. "It's too strong to fully dispel but..." The oppressive darkness dissipated as the magic in our immediate area cleared.

It didn't leave in our favor though. We appeared to be transported, chair included, to some sort of cave. Not much could be seen as the only light was a small lantern a short distance away. As I took in the lackluster surroundings I quickly saw 'us' was just me, Ash, and Cat. Worry gripped my chest. Where could the others be? Where were we?

Cat bit her lip as she took in everything. "The cold feels a lot like my step sisters' magic." She whispered softly.

We all stood up, as if that would give us better bearings on the situation at hand. No one looked happy. Confusion, concern, and dread passed through everyone's expressions before Ash nodded and finally spoke.

"That wasn't the magic that brought us here, though. It's too... melodic."

"What?" That didn't make sense to me.

"I've noticed more and more, raw magic has its own song, so to speak. Usually a basic spell is just a verse, a small part of the song. If I can just find the right note, I can unravel it. That should get rid of the ridiculous darkness, but the other magic, I can't tell where it's centered. It's far more complex."

Her magic was more unusual than anything I had encountered and I had learned early on not to question the strangeness of it. There just weren't many answers. "Think that'll work here?" It was the safest thing to ask.

Ash nodded, seemingly spacing out as her mind focused elsewhere. "I've found the pattern."

Cat breathed a sigh of relief. Her magic occasionally misfired but I knew overall she would be ready to handle whatever situation we ended up in. I just wondered what happened to the others?

The magic suddenly dispelled and we could see that we were in fact in a cave with only a small lantern left nearby.

Cat glanced around nervously as she summoned the lantern to her with her minor telekinetic talent. "I still sense her."

I looked around carefully, trying to remember what talents we all had. What talents did I even have? Illusions weren't exactly useful at this exact moment.

Ash let out a deep breath. "Arnessa, can you conjure up some better light?"

I nodded at her, glad one of us could think straight. I summoned up a handful of little fire lights and cast them around us, spreading our range of view. Sadly there wasn't much to see: cave walls and tunnels leading off further into the darkness. At least it wasn't damp. Just cold and musty.

Ash looked around approvingly. "Good start. Okay… What other useful things can we do?"

Cat let her stoneflesh magic cover her arms in scales. "I don't think we have much in the way of usefulness, but let's try to find our way out of here."

"Oh, I should check our location." Ash laughed, pulling her phone out of her pocket before frowning.

"No signal?" I guessed.

"Yeah, but I should always have a signal. My brother Marcus used his magic on my phone." Ash explained.

Cat frowned. "Didn't you say that happened when you met Nadia? His type of technology enchantments are beyond compare."

Ash nodded, more to herself than to us as she thought through things. "Exactly, but that was Daeum magic. This feels different."

I didn't like the sound of that. "Different how? Like it could be a different Daeum or something completely different altogether?"

Ash looked thoughtful for a moment. "Maybe it could be a different Daeum. Everything I've read makes it sound like there are a ton of them, but we haven't exactly done anything worth a Daeum's attention."

"Didn't you say when you were explaining it to us forever ago that they come to the calls they find most interesting?" I asked for confirmation. I knew the universe was a big place, so how could we, really Ash, encounter two Daeum's in just her lifetime?

Ash gave a nod. "That's correct. They do as they please, overall anyway. After going through the scrolls Nadia collected for me, I've uncovered a few more details, but nothing overly useful."

"Like what? Maybe there's a detail that will help us here?" I hoped there was anyway.

Ash sighed as she began to pace. "There is a hierarchy and system of rules for when encountering mortals. The hierarchy, as far as I can figure, is very, good witch, bad witch. The Noble beings are at the top. The ones that cause the most chaos, and actual negative mayhem are the Lesser Daeums. They tend to avoid the others, since well, if I read correctly, the Noble Daeum's pretty much instantly slay the Lesser. We believe that a Noble Daeum was who caused the situation with Nadia."

"What about the rules?" Cat inquired, her expression still as tight and stressed as when we first arrived. I noted that she kept looking toward the tunnels to my right.

"To gain access to their magic, one must accomplish something for them," Ash summed up before continuing on, pacing a circle around our immediate area. "According to what we learned from the council, they all gave up a minor magical talent in order to have their request met. After the objectives are completed, the

Daeum is allowed to take a bit of liberty in completing their goal but it isn't supposed to cause purposeful physical harm."

"Isn't supposed to?" That did not sound comforting.

"Well, a great example is Nadia's case. Being changed into a different form does not cause harm. Fighting the wolves guarding the area can, but that was a choice she made, not a choice the Daeum made for her. Though she had claws to help her stay safe enough. It's weird. Don't mess with deities." Ash shook her head, coming to a stop before pointing down a tunnel. "I sense the least amount of magic that way."

Cat nodded, looking relieved it was in the opposite direction she had been eyeing. "Someone didn't get that memo about messing with them. Either way, that's away from the magic I sense, so let's try it."

I sighed, not liking the idea of wandering, but it was better than waiting here. "Let's give it a go then."

I created a handful of little fire lights to follow us, creating a magical trail so if we had to backtrack, we could.

Cat and Ash walked ahead, nearly side by side as I trailed behind. I made sure a light stayed several paces ahead of them but wasn't exactly sure what we could encounter. My body felt rigid as I thought of bears, and other creatures with claws and teeth.

After several deadends and a lot of backtracking, those fears stopped. We were more bored than not, wandering with a faint hope of finding an exit.

"Could we be trapped?" I finally mused aloud as we came to a halt at a crossway.

"I wouldn't be surprised at this point." Cat agreed, no longer tense or concerned.

"There has to be a way…" Ash sighed, picking a path and continuing to walk. "If it is Daeum magic, we can't be stuck without food, or water, or everything…"

"Didn't you say this felt different?" Cat asked hesitantly as we followed.

I didn't like the direction that thought was going. "What if this is from a Lesser Daeum?"

Ash stopped dead in her tracks and tilted her head to the side, as if she was listening to something.

We watched her for a moment before Cat spoke up. "You okay there, Ash?"

Ash turned to face us. "Oh, am I the only one who can hear that?"

"Hear what?" I was starting to worry about her.

"That sound…" She trailed off and nodded toward the wall.

I looked at it, puzzled for a moment before I let my magic flow. The illusion was so tight knit I wouldn't have noticed it without her mentioning it.

"It's mixed with magic I'm not familiar with. Can you do something about that?" I asked Ash as Cat stared at us like we were both losing it.

"Hmmm." Ash thought aloud.

After a few moments, maybe even a full minute I felt something change. I pulled at it with my magic, caressing all the threads of the illusion before tearing it to shreds and unveiling another pathway.

"Well, this can't be good." Cat shook her head. "Shall we go anyway?" She motioned to the new tunnel before leading the way.

"Might as well." Ash agreed, touching part of the wall. "Going to mark this and let that magic flow again in case whoever, or whatever, brought us here checks back."

I nodded as I followed and was surprised that the illusion quickly mended once Ash did her thing. If it was a Daeum, I wondered what magical characteristic Ash shared with them to be able to do that. Some magics overlapped. Her brother Marcus was an easy example. He could enchant and manipulate any technology like a master enchanter could, but he could also go beyond, only with that niche ability though.

I didn't voice my curiosity; for now, we needed to focus on getting out. I just hoped the others were okay and faring better than we were.

CHAPTER TWO

----Nadia----

Vincent lit a small fireball in his hand as we all sat in silent surprise at the suddenly dark room. Magical lights didn't just go out. We looked around at one another, not sure what to say about the odd problem when it dawned on us.

"Where is everyone?" Rey shot up from his chair, Vincent shortly behind him.

I didn't move. Instead, I let my shifting magic rise and inhaled deeply, trying to see if my wolf could gather anything useful. Trails would be easy enough to pick up on.

"They're not here." I said, shocked by the realization. "Their scent just ends where they were sitting." That didn't make any sense. How could someone come in, with no scent and take them without a trace?

"You're saying someone just magicked them away? Into thin air?" Vincent asked, mouth agape. I could feel him stretching out his magic, searching for illusions.

"That is exactly what I'm saying." I confirmed, glancing over at Rey who stared at me in horror.

"What? Why them?" Rey asked, not able to come up with a reason.

My best guess wasn't much of an answer. "Likely to get our attention. It would be a huge national emergency for them to take us." I looked over at Vincent. "You're due to wed in about a month correct?"

Vincent nodded. "Yeah, so this would still cause an uprise. There might be another reason."

"I can't think of one. Cat and I just got engaged after the new year. You're not engaged yet, are you?" Rey looked to me for confirmation.

"Not yet. Finding the right moment is harder than I thought." I sighed. "Not that it matters now."

Vincent closed his eyes and the darkness vanished as he dismantled the spell. "Whatever was making it impossible to remove the illusion a moment ago is gone."

I bit my lip as I considered that. "What could make it impossible to remove an illusion? You're a master level enchanter, are you not?"

Vincent nodded. "Certified and everything." he confirmed. That exam wasn't easy to pass. The series of tests took months to go through.

"Can anything block that?" Obviously there could be since it happened, but what?

"Nothing comes to mind. It would have to be ungodly powerful." He sighed, coming up as blank as I had.

Oh.

Oh no.

"Not this again." I leaned forward into my hands, groaning, before taking a deep breath and facing them.

"What does that mean?" Rey raised an eyebrow at me, surprised and confused by my dramatics.

"Possibly another Daeum issue. We lost my little bookworm to whatever is happening, though." I explained, trying not to sound too exasperated by the likely turn in events.

Rey looked tired as he thought. "Ash sent me a lot of that information since I thought it sounded cool but I'd be lying if I said I read more than half of it. I know Cat read over a bit, but that's not exactly helpful right now."

Helpful was exactly what we needed right now. I pulled out my phone and started to search my contacts. "Let's see if Marcus can find them."

Vincent and Rey audibly sighed in relief. Marcus had gained a lot of popularity in our group with his tech magic. Everything was so much easier when someone could magically transform your things.

He picked up on the second ring and I quickly filled him in on the little that happened before putting him on speaker phone. Before I could even ask him to, Marcus was already typing away in the background and then quickly cursing.

"It's exactly how things were with the Daeum situation." he finally snarled before letting another string of curses out. "Wait… there's…" he muttered to himself for a moment. "You're never going to believe this."

"What is it?" Vincent demanded.

"A weird box popped up. It says to find the ones you miss the most, return back to the beginning in a week's time." Marcus replied. "Whatever is going on, I really don't think you should do that. Not yet anyway."

"What is that even supposed to mean?" Rey grumbled, but I had a feeling.

"Someone must be very mad at us." I said simply.

"What do you mean?" Vincent seemed surprised. Not that the goodie-two-shoes did much wrong.

Marcus gave a laugh. "Oh that is very, very likely."

At least Marcus seemed to be on the same page. "Well," I began, "They took those who are very close to us. I'm going to guess the beginning has to do with them. Was there someone you may have accidentally wronged where our loves are concerned?"

The two men in front of me groaned.

"I don't even know where to begin with that." Vincent finally grumbled after a moment passed. "I know Arnessa's step family really hates her. They aren't even invited to the wedding at this point."

Rey nodded. "Yeah, I'm fairly certain Cat's family found out through the grapevine about the engagement. It's not really her fault, though. Don't think any of this is really anyone's fault."

"Depends on who you ask." I hated where my own thoughts were going. "Those who feel wronged like to hold grudges and will hold whatever view they like, as incorrect as it may be."

"I really don't think Arnessa's family is clever enough to pull something like this off, though." Vincent shook his head.

"I really don't expect this from Cat's family either." Rey agreed.

I folded my hands in front of me, "I wish I could say the same."

"What do you mean by that? Ash gets along great with her brother." Vincent sounded as perplexed as Rey looked.

"Isn't her mother gone, and father well out of the picture? That doesn't make any sense." Rey agreed with Vincent's statement.

"Let me tell you about a little thorn named Donny." I said.

Marcus started laughing, more annoyed than amused. I had forgotten he was still on speaker. "A little thorn named Donny is a great way to start the story. I'll do some digging on what he's been up to."

"Thank you, Marcus." That would speed things up. "While you're at it, can you check in on all the possible families? Might as well see if any of them are involved."

"Already running that." He chuckled.

"You're the man." Vincent cheered.

With a sigh, I gave them the brief run down about what I knew about Donny from Ash and Marcus, and the little bit I experienced. It was too bad he didn't get locked up for longer and sadly, restraining orders were just paper.

"Well, any leads yet or is it too soon?" I asked Marcus hopefully as I finished.

"Actually, already getting information you're not going to like." Marcus said. His grim tone said enough, and yet we still needed the facts.

"I don't feel like this situation is going to have any real ups until it's resolved." Rey sighed, speaking accurately for all of us.

"Donny wasn't seen in town for about seven months. Just straight up vanished according to most people. Says on social media he was on a hunting trip. According to records I shouldn't have access to but may have gotten access to, he did a lot of traveling. He seemed to go off the grid a continent over and showed up again on a completely different continent before using any ID or cards again." There was a lot of rapid typing and clicking going on as he spoke. "It's confirmed that he has been back in Arnessa's hometown as well as Cat's."

"Damn, didn't think someone like him could travel like that." Rey whistled.

"It gets better." Marcus said dryly.

Vincent groaned as he covered his face. "Well, let's hear it."

"Donny has been missing for the last month again. Recent reports were from Arnessa's family coffee shop, and just before that a coffee shop near Cat's. So, the best place to start looking for him is at that coffee shop. Sadly, all video feed seems to be missing from those visits. I don't know what you'd find if you asked in person, but you should have people for that."

Nadia clicked her tongue. "Who's to say those people aren't all gone? In fact, if this is a Daeum at work, I bet everyone we could use to help us is temporarily gone."

Vincent pulled out his phone. "I really hope you're wrong."

I couldn't tell who he was calling, but it didn't matter. No one had rushed to us when the power went out so I doubted I was wrong, at least as far as my own people went.

After a moment he shook his head. "Okay, no one's answering but they all might be busy with dinner."

Rey pulled out his phone. "Mother would totally answer her phone for me, dinner or not." We waited expectantly. "Okay, four rings is very troubling. She's answered in two rings in the middle of the night before." When no one picked up, he slammed his phone on the table. "What now?"

"Well Marcus, am I right in guessing we should have a direction to go in? Daeums just love giving a very specific set of rules." I really didn't want this to be a Daeum, but it seemed that was exactly who we were dealing with.

Marcus sighed deeply. "Well, we didn't until you said something. I'm going to read exactly what this new popup says and let me tell ya, it's fun."

"The joy is all ours." Vincent grumbled as he crossed and uncrossed his arms, too agitated to get comfortable.

"Go for it." I agreed, gesturing into the void.

"All ears." Ray gave a slight nod.

"Here we go." Marcus took a breath before reading it. "Your presence is not requested at this time. If you try and seek who you lost, in an endless maze you'll reside. Stay put and wait, don't rush, just hesitate. Let the threats be removed, and the guy try to swoon."

"That freaking asshole!" I shouted. I didn't need more details. "Donny had to have been the one to try and set this whole mess up! And since he couldn't possibly do it all on his own he tried to get more people involved in this mess."

"So, he picked other people that might have a thing against royals?" Rey asked, exasperated. "None of this makes sense."

"He'd have to have half a brain to make sense!" I tried to rein in my voice, but it was hard to hold back my anger. I couldn't help but snarl in my wolf growl causing both guys to take a half step back.

"It's okay, we'll figure this out. Somehow." Vincent tried to reassure me, but his words lacked conviction.

"If we try to find them, worse will happen! But we can't stand by and wait!" I pounded my fists on the table causing everything on it to rattle.

"Actually, it just says we'll give up in a maze, in stupid fancy wording." Rey pointed out. "So we may still get some really good information before that point. It might be worth it to look."

"I bet they're counting on you to sit back since you know how Daeum's work." Vincent agreed.

My temper cooled some. "True…" I wasn't sure what to think, but I really needed to keep my anger in check.

"I don't think you need my help from here, but" Marcus interjected, "Don't divide this up. Stay as a group. I'm sure they'll be expecting you to divide and conquer if you do go out, and they'll likely have a way to counter your magic."

Rey nodded. "I agree. Do you have information about everyone's magic? That'll be useful in case we do get into some sort of squabble."

"I'm sending you each an email with all those details, what the pop-ups were, and everything else I can find." Marcus replied with a chuckle. "Check back regularly."

"Thank you Marcus. Don't know what we'd do if you disappeared." I meant it too. We'd be lost right now.

Marcus gave another laugh. "I'm betting those families and Donny told the Daeum who the greatest threats are. In his eyes, I'm the useless tech guy. Brains over brawn wins this round."

"Thanks man." Rey said, already looking at his phone. "This is perfect."

"No problem. I'll see what else I can do to help. Find my sister and kick his ass Nadia." Marcus called to me.

"Gladly." I agreed. I was more than ready to solve this, and potentially remove someone's arms, but that would have to wait until we found Donny.

We made plans and gathered provisions before we started out early the next morning. Using the full advantage of magical travel and royal privilege, we made it to Magic Beans shortly after their morning rush. None of us were exactly sure how to approach the situation, and we really only had the most basic of plans.

"So, I can change everyone's appearance with my illusions, but what exactly should we say?" Vincent asked as we eyed the shop hesitantly. With a shrug I felt his magic cover us, disguising us in an instant.

"I've no idea, but I can have my wards at the ready in case we are attacked with anything magical." Rey offered as we stood outside at the very end of the lot.

"I wish diplomacy worked with deities. No one deserves this sort of situation." I tried to think of what tactics might work. "If worse comes to worse, I suppose I can just scare it out of them."

Rey's lips turned up with amusement. "Think they'll be afraid of the big bad wolf?"

"Wouldn't you be?" I flashed an extra toothy smile and noted the falter in his smile.

"Yeah, I think I would be." Rey agreed, shaking it off.

"While I love backups, we really need an actual plan." Vincent pointed out as we looked at the shop. We had as much of a solid plan as last night. It was almost infuriating how terrible we were at this.

"You all suck at hiding." a voice said, causing us to turn. "Even disguised, I guessed just by the conversation."

A girl I did not recognize stood with her arms crossed, a bored look on her face.

"Oh, Rose, was not expecting you to be out here." Vincent supplied, his voice sounding uneasy but his posture looking as confident as ever.

I could only guess this was one of the step sisters.

"So, like, you're all here because Diamond and mom are being total snob trolls who can't lose anything." Rose said as if it were the most obvious thing in the universe.

"Um, basically?" Vincent looked both confused and surprised. He gave a small laugh to offset his unease. "Anything you can help us with?"

"Yeah, I probably can, but it's a total boring waste of time. So what's in it for me?" Rose may have been young, but she still knew enough to play this to her advantage. While it annoyed me, I couldn't exactly fault her for it.

"What do you want?" I asked bluntly. "I'd rather not waste time. Money or some spotlight are easy enough grabs if that's what you're looking for. Name the price."

Rose looked at me curiously. "Here's the thing; since Nessa left, the shop has been failing. I hate the place, and Di can't do a damn thing since she's useless. But that means there's no money for fun and important things, and I want to go to the Talarium Academy. I was good enough for an invite, but not a scholarship."

We all seemed to be a bit surprised.

"Done. Consider your dance school paid for." If the kid wanted to dance, so be it. I had instructors from there on and off growing up, and knew what it meant for a dancer to attend there.

Rose gave a single nod before smiling. "Perfect. The important things you need to know are mom and Di have amulets that can dispel illusions. Cat's stepsister has a sword that can break stoneflesh and cause a lot of physical harm; her nasty step mom didn't want to get her hands dirty, so she's out of the picture. That annoying Donny guy, though, is a real pain and has arrows that never miss their target. They're poisoned, I guess. Maybe, like, seven minutes and you die or something."

"That's pretty awful. How did they even get all this stuff?" Rey shook his head.

"Some magic lady from space." Rose shrugged. "She's like a super mad wicked witch, and pure chaos and stuff." Rose gestured vaguely. "She, like, um has rules, but like doesn't have to play by them all? Just as long as like she goes unnoticed enough, she can get away with a billion things before she needs to vanish."

Well, that wasn't a good sign.

"Thanks Rose." Vincent nodded with some relief.

"Anything else we should be aware of? Or any idea where they're being kept?" Rey asked hopefully.

Rose looked thoughtful for a moment. "It's that unicorn place but they're like, in this loop thing so even if they find the exit they'll keep walking in a giant circle."

"Unicorn place?" Unicorns aren't real. Well, at least I hadn't thought they were. I guess if Daeum's were a thing, why not magical horses.

"Yeah…" Rose did not sound interested in the least. "I don't know where it is. That annoying Donny guy with the IQ of two squirrels glued together somehow found it, but of course won't tell us. I hardly believe him though. Come on, for reals. We've got a freaking absurd amount of magical people and there is just no way we'd not have found them by now, ya know?"

I wasn't going to mention I was hidden from the entire world both physically, and in memory, for about nineteen months. Instead I kept it simple "Yeah, that guy does have an IQ of two squirrels glued together, doesn't he?"

Rose gave an agreeing nod. "Anyway, that's all I know. Good luck with that stuff. Now, that school thing?" She stared at me expectantly.

"Of course. You have my word. Sadly, this space lady nonsense has hidden all my people, but…" I pulled out my phone. "What is your contact information?"

Rose held out her hand. Reluctantly I handed over my phone and she put in her number and email. "There you have it." She handed it back. "When this resolves, I expect everything to be immediately taken care of."

"Agreed." She had solved a fair amount of our problems before we could even put together a game plan. It was the least I could do. The least any of us could do.

"Now, if you'll excuse me, I've got work to fashionably be late to." Rose said as she headed toward the building.

"Should we tell her you can't be fashionably late to work?" Vincent muttered.

"Don't you dare." Rey tried to hold back a laugh. "We have half this matter figured out now."

"But not the where." I pointed out.

"Well, we sort of do. It has to be one of those places that Donny guy disappeared to." Rey countered.

"Yeah, maybe Marcus has figured something out. I bet he looked into those locations already." Vincent agreed.

"Marcus needs to sleep sometime." I didn't have a real counter.

"Yeah, but his sister is missing, again, so I bet anything he's stayed up all night trying to uncover as many details as physically possible." Vincent pulled out his phone. "He did say he'd keep us updated."

"I'm pretty sure tech and gamer people don't really sleep anyway." Rey gave a slight chuckle.

"And he did find something!" Vincent smiled for a moment. "It looks like it involves a lot of hiking though."

"Of course it would." I shook my head. "Let's go somewhere a bit safer. I don't trust staying here any longer."

"Agreed. We've done the deed, let's get going." Rey glanced over at the shop before we headed away.

CHAPTER THREE

----Cat----

What a mess we'd landed ourselves in. I wasn't sure why anyone would want us. While Arnessa and I were engaged to royalty, and Ash just about there herself, we weren't exactly the most exciting bunch. I had a great job making enchanted things, but overall I was just a gamer nerd a bit too obsessed with niche things.

I wouldn't say the other two were much different. Arnessa had her painting, and Ash had probably read a library's worth of books just this year alone. Of course, we all did some form of gaming, hence the roleplay group monthly meetup. If it was money they wanted, they were certainly barking up the wrong tree. While they may get the funds for a while, in the end, they'd be caught. I couldn't imagine the sentence for this level of crime.

But what if it was this Daeum being that Ash thought it was?

Would they just mess around with us until the person who summoned them had their goals met? What could those goals be? I was confident Melanie was still bitter on several fronts, but aside from not getting the prince she was terribly unsuited for, nothing bad actually happened to her. We broke ties. I hadn't spoken to her since the incident where she tried to attack me when I was moving out. I couldn't imagine why she would still waste energy and effort to go after me, but I knew that magic, and she was somewhere around here.

I didn't think the others doubted me when I said that, but there was so much magic going on. I wondered why they would pick a cave system to stick us in. Honestly, that answer might be the easiest to come by. I highly doubted Melanie would explain her hand in this mess. Maybe there was something more going on here that I was missing. I shook my head as if that would be enough to clear this mess away and instead tried to focus on the danger at hand.

The hidden tunnel we found after hours of searching ended up being just the right ticket and got us outside. A forest greeted us just a few yards from the cave entrance and a large rocky hillside was at our backs. Thankfully, there were normal forest sounds going on around us so we likely weren't being pursued or hunted. At least not by anything to startle the animals and insects into hiding. Wherever this place was, the sun was just now setting.

"We're not on Caslein anymore are we?" I commented. It was nice to step away from the cave and breathe fresh air. Cozy, slightly warm air at that. It was getting chillier at night back home as fall started to show its colors. That didn't seem to be the case here.

Ash and Arnessa both looked at the sky and the slowly setting sun, shielding their eyes from the few bright rays remaining.

"It doesn't look like it." Arnessa agreed, turning to me. "We were wandering long enough for it to be dark back home."

"We're going to need to rest soon." Ash said as she pulled out her phone. "Nothing. No service. No time update." She sighed. "Maybe we're on Pangwen?"

"That lines up with my guess." Arnessa nodded, taking in the surroundings. "It's beautiful here. I wish I had my sketchpad."

I had no opinion. It didn't matter where we were until we found a way to reach people anyway. I'm sure they were freaking out by now. Hopefully they weren't in a worse situation.

"Where should we camp out?" I wondered aloud.

"I don't know if the tunnel is technically safer or not. We don't know what's out here." Ash glanced around. "We don't know what lives in there either so…"

"I'd rather be out than in." Arnessa said firmly, putting her hands on her hips. "I can create an illusion so nothing bothers us, so that should be safe enough. I'd rather avoid cave creatures."

"We should set a watch just in case. While illusions won't have anything purposefully bother us, something could accidentally." I really hated sleeping outside, but that cave was giving me more anxiety than the engagement photoshoot I did two months ago. I hated proper, fancy dresses, but I would deal with that before possibly encountering my step-sister again.

"That sounds reasonable." Ash walked in a slow circle around us. "But where do we set up? What if it gets too cold?"

I hadn't thought about that. My stone flesh actually was fairly insulating.

"I've got nothing useful for that." Arnessa frowned.

"Maybe your magic will help if that's the case?" I suggested to Ash.

Ash gave a shrug. "It's not impossible." She had set a few things on fire before.

The magical category she was in was rare, annoying, and exceedingly unreliable. Even if I accidentally blew things up, at least I had that option. Sometimes Ash couldn't even get her magic to do that much.

"Okay, let's set up a camp I guess." I motioned vaguely around. "This will probably be the best area. We can climb up this bit of hillside in the daylight and get a better perspective on things."

"Great idea. Have you camped a lot?" Arnessa seemed impressed.

I shook my head. "It's what I'd do in my games honestly."

Ash gave a small laugh. "Well, if it works, then why not."

Arnessa walked over to the hillside but gave the mouth of the cave a wide berth. "Here I guess?" We all joined her and I could feel magic shroud us. It was comforting at least, even if it just upped our stealth.

"Do you still feel your step-sister's magic?" Ash asked quietly as we settled into our hiding spot.

I shook my head. "I haven't felt it since we found the passage out of here. There was a lot of it but I can't tell if she just had a hand in setting things up, or if she was actually hidden in there."

"Maybe both." Arnessa shrugged. "If she teamed up with my step-sisters' friend, I bet they could cause the right amount of chaos. Adding in a Daeum would make things even worse."

"I just wonder what could have been asked for that would get a Daeum's attention." Ash shook her head tiredly. "The last time I encountered one with Nadia was confusing. The council had one member wanting a happily ever after, a fairytale ending to a terrible situation, and that one call was heard. Something in their phrasing was enough."

"So, good or bad, whatever weird phrasing this Daeum caught wind of was enough to catch their interest," I sighed. "But we don't know the way out. Isn't there a rule where we're supposed to know what's going on?"

"Not if it's a Lesser Daeum. They skirt the rules at best." Ash laid down and looked up at the clear sky as stars began to show in the slowly growing darkness.

I nodded, remembering some of it from the files she sent me. "What rules will it abide by?" My words came out more quiet than I intended and I wasn't sure if anyone heard them.

"The cave is likely the safe place we were meant to reside. That's probably the only rule they're guaranteed to follow." Ash replied, equally quiet.

Be trapped in safety or less secure in freedom? None of us suggested to move back inside. Being stuck in there wasn't worth it.

"Let's try and rest." A yawn escaped my lips as I stretched out.

With little more to discuss, we quickly set a schedule and tried to sleep.

The last watch was Arnessa's. She claimed her body was used to being up early anyway, and I honestly wasn't going to argue with that logic. As the sky started to lighten again, she nudged us awake. I tried to bite back a grumble as I remembered where we were. Mornings were not my thing, but I wasn't going to be a troll about it out here. As I started to really wake up, I realized why she woke us. Something didn't feel right, something very strongly magical at that. Scales covered my skin from the neck down as everything registered.

"What is it?" Ash asked in a soft voice before I could.

"I don't know." Arnessa admitted. "I can't see anything, but there's no mistaking something is here."

I bit the bottom of my lip. "I could try and draw it out. Use my telekinesis… at least we'd know what it is." I hoped.

Arnessa shook her head. "I don't know if I want to know. If we can feel it this strongly and not see it, it's already easy to avoid."

"I wish that were the case…" Ash whispered, the words barely reached my ears.

"What do you mean?" I dropped my voice even lower to match hers.

"We're surrounded." she said in awe.

Arnessa looked around surprised. "I don't sense anything that close…"

Ash gave a small, almost defeated laugh. "It's not normal illusion magic."

It clicked with me, the magic feeling more akin to my stoneflesh gifts. The magic was much more land based, but not somehow. As if the magic was pulled from the very core of the earth and not just the land itself.

"It's so… earthy, but not." I remarked lamely, my thoughts providing me with zero alternative phrasing.

Arnessa continued to look around, her frown deepening. "I can illusion, I can brew, and I can conjure. This is well out of my realm."

Ash sighed. "Let's see…"

I turned to face her as her entire being softly glowed red and orange before turning a brilliant blue and suddenly the area around us changed, ever so slightly, revealing the truth. We were in fact surrounded, and never in my life did I suspect or believe I could be encircled by a group of unicorns.

"This would be so much cooler if they were a little less stabby." I blurted, more in awe than fear. "They're so pretty…"

"*Thank you,*" I heard a voice say.

We all jumped in surprise. I couldn't tell which one said it.

"*What is a group of two humans doing here?*" another voice asked.

"We really don't know…" Ash shrugged. "But I assume you can count so why did you say two? There's three of us?"

The unicorns looked among themselves and seemed to nod at one another.

"*A group who shouldn't be here has arrived in the heart of our land. How interesting. What can you tell us about your journey here?*" the first voice asked again.

I finally pinpointed who was talking, but it was clear they didn't speak with their mouths the way I originally guessed.

I didn't know if we should trust them with the details, but they had the upper hand, both magically and physically. Still, I hesitated and Ash looked just as reluctant.

"We were at a friend's..." Arnessa answered carefully, unsure what details to provide. "There were six of us playing a game when the power went out. When we tried to break the illusion we found ourselves in a cave here. We don't know what happened to the others. Hopefully they are still at home."

The group of unicorns looked from one to another once more.

"We're sorry for accidentally ending up in your lands. We really just want to get home," Ash assured, calmly. "Can you point us in a direction that might help us get there?"

They didn't acknowledge her statement in any way and seemed to be quietly communicating among themselves.

"We can't just simply leave, can we?" I finally asked after a beat.

I got a few tilted heads before the first one replied to me again, *"No, there is much magic tied to you that will take time to unthread. Then you'll need to forget this place before we can send you back."*

"What! Why?" Arnessa just about shouted. She didn't seem angry, just confused, and likely not wanting anyone to mess with her mind. I sided with her on that, but what choice would we even have?

"It is for everyone's safety." the unicorn replied. *"Your kind likes to take advantage of our magic, and we can too easily wipe out most of your kind. We're content to stay in our lands if you leave us be. History has proven this to be the best way."*

I nodded. That made complete sense to me, and there were too many books, movies, and games that strongly reiterated that fact. While some societies could live in peace, humans were often the reason for trouble. I wouldn't even try to argue it.

"What sort of magic is threaded around us?" Ash asked curiously. "I was concerned a Daeum was trying to manipulate things."

"It is." the unicorn confirmed. *"Why this one put you here we cannot tell. We have an understanding with this particular one. They show up again, and they die."*

That was unexpected and unsettling.

"What did they do?" I couldn't help but ask, the words were out of my mouth before I could even consider how nosy they were.

"*That is too much information for you.*" came the reply.

"But if we're not going to remember anyway, what does it matter?" Arnessa tried to reason, letting curiosity get the better of her as well.

"I'll take a wild stab here that something about them has highly magical properties that even a Daeum would want to take advantage of." Ash supplied. "So, what do we have to do to get home? As neat as this all is, I know I have some very concerned people waiting to hear from me. I'd rather not know what they'll do to try and reach me."

The unicorns seemed amused, several even appeared to be smirking, if that was possible for them.

"*Then magic home.*" the first unicorn said in a light, entertained tone.

"My magic doesn't do that." Ash frowned, looking at us to see if we got what was so funny.

"*It does.*" the unicorn nickered, as if it were laughing.

Ash looked like she wanted to argue but paused. "Wait, do you understand my magic?"

"*Yes, why don't you?*" There was a bit more nickering, as if Ash should know her magic. As if it wasn't complicated.

"Because it's not understood. Very few with my magic have mastery over it." Ash said, her words almost mirroring my thoughts. "But you do and that doesn't make sense. None of the last twelve hours have made sense." She sighed, looking defeated.

"*Because your kind learns from ours.*" came the simple reply.

Arnessa and I glanced at Ash who stared at the group of unicorns with a look of pure 'you've got to be kidding me'.

"My kind? What is my kind? How would we learn from you if you're all hidden and everything?" Ash's frustration was starting to show and I could feel the magic bubbling up around her.

"*Breakfast first.*" With that the entire herd of unicorns turned and started walking away.

I looked from them back to Ash who was starting to glow gold. "Are you okay?" I asked softly, hoping not to accidentally provoke her magic.

"Far from it." she muttered, but the magic waned and vanished from view.

"At least they have answers." Arnessa tried to reassure her.

"But what will it take to get them?" Ash motioned toward the unicorns tiredly.

Now that was the real question.

CHAPTER FOUR

----Vincent----

When we first started to regularly meet up, mother was worried someone would try and target the group. I had laughed it off, as did Arnessa. Who would really try and take on a group of mages that were extremely powerful in their fields?

Apparently the correct answer was a deity.

My illusions made zero difference here. Neither did my enchanting in the long run. My destruction magic was good, but it wasn't better than any college grad in that field so I doubted it would do much here. Still, it was more than infuriating to be messed with.

And they stole my fiance!

Stupid god like being messing with my life. I had found the perfect girl, became acquainted with an amazing friend group, and just when life couldn't get much better, everything plummeted off the face of a cliff.

Mom probably didn't realize she'd be right in this particular way, but I fully deserved that 'I told you so' and the smack on the shoulder she'd give me. We had to solve this, and quickly. Not just for my mental well being either. Nadia was one wrong word away from shifting into a dire wolf and annihilating the next idiot to talk to her. I couldn't blame her though. Even Rey who was normally too carefree to be human was tense and ready to pop.

The good news was Marcus figured out several things after running some bots and getting friends to search for Donny's location. After some airport footage and security cameras from random places, Marcus figured the jerk had gone to Pangwen several times over, always heading toward the Eethar Peak trail. We couldn't figure out why, but every time he showed up with different hunting and tracking equipment.

Still, people didn't go there for a laundry list of reasons, primarily the weird magic that made people disappear. Some would show up months later on another continent with no memories, but those were the lucky ones. I remember reading that while everyone did gain back most of their memories, no one remembered the day before the mountains, the time they were gone, or anything before randomly appearing again.

The other place he visited frequently was on Kiwanii. He got stopped at customs for having weird animal fur, but after a while it was determined to be wolf fur and was sent off with it. He claimed it was werewolf. The shifter community has always stated that it was a myth. Magic didn't work that way. You had a bloodline that transformed into one animal, or the ability to shift into several of a certain mass.

Whatever that Donny guy was up to, he was clearly losing his mind more and more. The pieces of which were now littering several continents. The one thing that couldn't be answered was how he convinced anyone to magic our girls away. Donny didn't have interesting magic. Marcus looked it up for us, or likely already knew from their last series of encounters. Donny was a master tracker, and could use magic to identify what made each trail. He could also change his vision to see at better distances, but not nearly as well as binoculars could. Aside from those niche gifts, he wasn't noteworthy. Donny was a D student who sometimes pulled off a C. He was also caught cheating several times so even those higher marks were likely lies.

Marcus had a needlessly long file on the guy, and every detail seemed to get more and more boring after he completed basic schooling. Why would anyone listen to him?

I asked Nadia as we started traveling and she just laughed. "Why do Daeum's listen to anyone? We are but ants. Make enough noise, build up enough nonsense, maybe even light a fire and you'll eventually get *someone's* attention. Why him? Probably, as you would say, for the lolz. They were likely already in the mood to cause some chaos and Donny is easy to play around with.

He'd listen to anything they say just for a chance at what he wants."

"I don't know who we should feel more sorry for if that's the case -him or us." I shook my head. "Having a Daeum play around with you cannot end well."

"Us." Rey scoffed. "If he was dumb enough to poke a sleeping giant, then let him. I hope this ends badly for him. Terrible even."

"I just hope it doesn't end badly for us as well." That was my biggest worry. Even if we tried all we could, and did everything right, what if we didn't really win? Could we get them all back? Were they even on this plane if a Daeum whisked them away?

"It's difficult to say. This one hasn't presented real rules, just teasing guidelines they expect us to follow." Nadia sighed.

"How did you find out your rules?" Rey asked before I could.

Nadia fidgeted with her sleeve as she replied. "Honestly, we all had a dream. I suppose the Daeum thought we'd be the most receptive to rules if we learned in our sleep. A blinding light told us while we were all dreaming. The rules were clearly laid out, the expectations equally so. We knew people could find and navigate the forest, it was just very unlikely anyone would."

"I'd take a blinding light with guidelines." Rey let out a long sigh. I couldn't agree more. This lack of anything felt ridiculous, and over the top movie villain-ish. Something needed to give, and quickly. We needed some form of hope.

I wished on every star I saw that things would turn out okay.

Travel was exhausting. Keeping us cloaked in an illusion for easier travel wasn't helping that end, but the weather was helping even less. The air was much more humid here, and the greenery only did so much to make up for the temperature. It was nice to be inside even after a brief trip from the airport to our hotel destination. We were eating dinner after traveling, trying to figure out our next move when Rey brought up a good point.

"Donny claimed to have werewolf fur when he was trying to board in Kaelin right?" Rey asked rhetorically. "And he also spent a lot of time in Pangwen, where we are now, presumably in the mountains where people regularly vanish."

"Yeah, so?" I wasn't sure why he was bringing that up. "That guy is losing it."

"Yeah, true, but what if the Daeum sent him here and there?" Rey said more than asked. "What if, the task he needed to complete in order for the Daeum's magic to work was to get these things that everyone believes is mythical, like the werewolf fur."

Nadia furrowed her brows as she thought. "That would be even more unpleasant and obnoxious for us. It would mean the Daeum needed mythical things for some reason, and that Donny would now know where to find everything should he ever so desire to again."

"You said there were two types of these deities right? How can we tell what one he summoned?" Rey continued on before Nadia could even answer. "What if there isn't something good to be learned or gained from this?"

"I don't even want to guess at anything you're implying." Nadia grumbled tiredly, rubbing her temples as a headache appeared to set in.

"Dude, this would be an epic campaign if it wasn't our lives." I sighed and stretched my arms out as I considered my own guess on his statement. "So, let's venture if it's not the good one trying to teach a lesson, it's the chaos one and just wants to bring disaster. Donny is the perfect match for someone who, if they can't have their way, will continue to use their new gained knowledge from the Daeum's tasks to continue to try to win a losing battle until the tides turn in his favor or he dies."

"That's the last thing I really want to consider with all of this." Nadia shook her head. "But it is likely. I can't find a shred of how this can be a *good* Daeum. Too many people are missing, kidnapped, and negatively impacted."

"So, what do we do when we find them?" Rey asked, poking at the last bit of food on his plate with his fork. "Is the Daeum going to be there? Are the crazy families following us? What if it's Donny? What if it's both?"

"I can hide us from Donny no problem." I shrugged knowing that on his own he wouldn't be able to break my illusions. "He's honestly not my biggest concern. That bow to always hit his target is only a problem for targets. If he can't see us, we're safe."

"That just leaves the Daeum." Nadia sighed. "Would help if I knew what one looked like."

"I still can't believe you've communicated with one and never saw them." Rey gave a tired laugh as he rubbed the sleep from his eyes.

"They appeared as a bright and blinding light so their true form was less startling or some crap." Nadia scoffed and crossed her arms. "If you ask me, they just didn't want to be seen. There's no way a being with that much magic couldn't make themselves appear in front of a mortal without being blinding or terrifying."

"I agree, that's really weird." It was an odd thing to ponder. "Unless they didn't want you to know who they were so they could continue to keep up with you in the future."

"Ha!" Nadia gave a short laugh at the idea. "Then they could look however else they wanted to!"

"But you'd know their magic." I countered. "If you were too blinded by the light to concentrate and really assess the situation, you got zero fix on them."

Nadia looked at me surprised. "Crap, you're completely right. That jerk." She went from surprised to enraged in less than a second. "I'm going to wring their neck if I ever see them again."

"You won't, they'll be too bright to see." Rey teased and Nadia hit him in the shoulder, hard, causing him to fall out of his chair.

I chuckled. "Well, at least we have a few things to sleep on. Let's get some rest. We have a lot of hiking even to reach the trail's border tomorrow."

"This would be so much more fun if we didn't have to hike there and back." Rey grumbled.

"Sounds like you boys need to get out into the woods more." Nadia snickered.

"We all can't go for moonlit runs as a wolf." Rey said drily. "So I think I'll stick with my games and lack of insects."

"Sounds boring." Nadia teased, getting up. "Goodnight then."

With quick goodnights, we separated. I was more than ready to have a few minutes alone. While I enjoyed my friends' company, I was too stressed and tired of vague planning to continue hanging out.

The second I entered my room the door behind me shut and everything went black.

"Not this again." I sighed as I summoned up a ball of fire in my hand.

The walls next to me were gone and it took me a longer second than I wanted to admit to realize I was floating and not standing.

I grumbled and accepted the nonsense around me. I wasn't sure what could surprise me anymore, and I really didn't want to be surprised at this point.

"So, um, what now?" I asked the darkened void.

"You're needed elsewhere first." a voice said simply.

Okay, that was more than I was expecting for a response. "Where and why?" Was that too much to ask? It seemed like easy answers were, in fact, too much to ask.

"You're needed to stop a mage." the voice replied and suddenly I fell a few inches into a cave.

I looked around surprised. "Where am I?"

"Stop the mage first." the voice replied. "The rest will come in time, but only if you stop the mage first. Do not deviate. Do not show yourself."

"Okay then." While it was straightforward, I felt more confused than I did floating in the void. With no more answers, I used my fire to get a good look around. Tunnels were here and there, and a feeling of cold magical essence. Was that who the voice meant? It wouldn't hurt to see since I had no other leads.

The second wind I was feeling was enough to keep me awake and I might as well make good use of this energy. Not that I had a choice. Apparently I needed to hunt down a rogue. I cast an illusion so no one would see me. Being invisible for now would be useful. The whole concept felt weird and off though. Why was I suddenly given instructions?

It struck me that maybe this wasn't the same Daeum. I wondered if we were right that the reason Nadia had no idea what the Daeum that bothered her looked like was because they were watching over her. Now we were all in a bind, and maybe that Daeum was still paying attention and lending just enough aid to guide us while not being involved enough for the other to know. Would the good Daeum take down the bad one? That would help us in the long run. Or was this just an amusing game for them both, with us like pawns at the center of a chess board? A good one may not be involved though, which was more likely. We were just on our own.

Knowing I wouldn't get an answer I closed my eyes and shut those thoughts out. Find the mage… There was magic coming from everywhere. The illusion magic was exactly like last night's when everyone vanished. I suspected that wasn't who I was being sent after. The only magic that felt different was that chilling ice magic.

I racked my brain for what that could mean when I remembered Rey and I late night ranting with each other about evil step-sisters. Cat's step-sister was equally vile compared to Diamond. The only exception was Diamond had very limited magic, whereas Melanie had reasonably obnoxious ice magic. This was likely her.

I slowly followed her trail of magic, the paths snaking and winding for what felt like eons until I reached a deadend. The illusion magic was weaker here, and I was able to dispel enough of it to walk through unhindered. It, of course, led to the continuation of a long winding tunnel.

Not much later I found a makeshift room with a girl sleeping in a small bed. Thankful, I had held in all the things I wanted to mutter angrily aloud. The magic radiated off of her even while she dreamt. I wasn't sure how to 'stop the mage' when they were doing nothing that needed to be stopped. At least nothing apparent. The most I could do was trap her mentally in an illusion but that was a pretty terrible thing to do for any length of time.

The answer dawned on me. I didn't need to magically stop her. We were up against people with weapons from a Daeum. If this was in fact Cat's stepsister, Melanie, then it would be best to remove the sword from the picture. It was the perfect idea. Of course she'd realize someone was on to her, but she'd have no way of knowing who or how without the Daeum's help. Even if the Daeum responded to her quickly, at least the sword would be out of the picture for a bit.

Slowly I moved and searched around the room, finding the sword under the bed. With nothing more to do, now felt like the best time to find my way out of this mess. Maybe I would find Arnessa and the others in the process.

I hoped with all my heart I would.

CHAPTER FIVE

----Rey----

This was not the adventure I asked for. I was beginning to assume I didn't like most real adventures and prefered every last one to be fictional. So, of course, life decided to ramp things up a notch and here I was, waking up not in the bed I fell asleep in. Nope. Instead I was waking up in the middle of a flipping field, with a goat licking my face.

The startling wakeup call left my heart racing and the rest of me thoroughly confused. Tall grass surrounded me, the only clear path being where the goat had walked through, stomping down some of the grass.

"Well, now what?" I muttered aloud to myself.

I got up and started to wander, the goat happily trailing behind me. The trail led to a clearing with a small house in the distance, and the mountain range I was supposed to be hiking toward just past that. I wondered if Nadia and Vincent were faring any better. This messy scenario was not what I wanted. It added to our already stressful adventure.

"While this looks cozy, none of this feels right…" I glanced over at the goat that had stopped along with me. "Well, what should I do now?"

The goat, of course, said nothing. A voice from behind startled me. "Swap the amulets."

I turned, but saw no one.

"I beg your pardon?" I hoped whoever spoke would reveal themselves.

"Swap the amulets." the voice repeated.

A clanking sound came from behind me, causing me to spin around to see two amulets laying in front of the goat.

Whatever was going on, at least the voice had told me what it expected. Ah, a Daeum. It had to be the helpful one. The Noble one or whatever they called themselves. That was all that made sense; after all the other didn't exactly bother with instructions. Sure, there was that message to Marcus, but really, it could have just applied to him. There was no direct communication with us.

I glanced at my horned companion wondering if they would follow me on this mission. That would make it extra difficult, but nothing so far had been too easy.

Sort of.

I guess Marcus did hand us almost all the information. Rose also gave us a lot of intel too, which reminded me that Arnessa's crazy stepsister Diamond and her mom had the weird amulets.

With a sigh I directed my attention back at the goat. "Listen, bud, I know you understand me, so I want you to understand that I can't have you following me around. Got it?"

The goat tilted his head to the side. *"Food?"* Well, that wasn't much different than communicating with my dogs back home.

"No, no food. You've got an entire field to devour. Go on, shoo." I motioned for it to stop following me.

It bleated at me, annoyed, before turning around and heading off. *"Where food?"* Well, at least that was one thing resolved. Now to figure out how to switch the amulets.

I could only guess that the house hidden nearby was where I needed to go. It was likely Donny had been using it while trying to do things out here, and was now being used as a base by the step-evils. Here we freaking go, I guess.

I walked into the edge of the forest along the side of the house, hoping that it would at least offer some sort of stealth while I tried my best to figure out the situation. As I got close, I was able to see the windows were open. From the sound of it someone was inside singing, and badly at that.

I cringed as I listened, waiting for a good moment to get closer, or even better, for the people inside to head out, preferably without said amulets. After several painstaking minutes, an actual conversation started. They sounded as if they were deeper in the house so I moved closer to the window to listen.

"This is totes pointless." a younger girl, I assumed Diamond, complained.

"Patience will reward us." an older, firmer voice, I was going with Stepmomster, replied.

"But like why wait here? What if they just go a different direction, ya know?" Diamond pointed out.

While I had zero idea what the bigger picture was here, she had a great point. No matter where anyone was located, this was a pretty big forest. Who would stumble upon them here?

"We were instructed to wait. They'll get us into position when the time is right, so we will never be in the wrong spot. We're just, how you say, in limbo. Waiting on the sidelines. Things should be changing soon enough." Her voice sounded confident, and somehow slimy. I didn't like anything about this woman and I hadn't exactly met her yet.

Still, yes, please! Continue with the details.

"Ugh, but this is la-A-ame." Diamond huffed in exaggeration. "Nessa just needs a quick whack to the head, lose her memory, and life will be grand once more."

"Indeed. She just had to run off instead of serving the family like a good daughter." Stepmomster's voice oozed with disappointment.

"Right? Her place was the shop. It's not even that hard to know your place. Stupid Nessa." Diamond groaned. "I need to go somewhere. Something. This place is snoozeville."

Yes! Go somewhere, wicked family. These people were really weirding me out and I didn't like the idea of them trying to make someone lose their memory. I wondered how Arnessa even put up with them as long as she did.

"No, we wait here. That idiot Melanie has already lost the sword. We cannot afford to have anything happen here. That being will not just give us new amulets." the Momster replied curtly.

"Not my fault Mel is stupid." Diamond mumbled.

"It's not, but she was supposed to be trailing the captives. How they got out of the tunnels, and with the sword no less, is a mystery. We cannot afford to lose the amulets as well." Momster was overtly firm in her words.

That sounded like good news overall, but bad news for me. The sword that could cut through even stoneflesh was missing, but how would I get the amulets now? Would they be wearing them? Was I going to have to wait until nightfall?

Of course now was probably the worst possible time for my new goat buddy to show up, but show up he did. He happily trotted up as I motioned for him to leave.

"Food?" Of course that's all he cared about. Goats were bottomless pits.

"I don't have food." I let my magic work, the mental communication working with ease. An idea struck as I connected with the goat. *"But they have food inside. A lot of good food."*

The goat tilted his head to the other side and then back again. *"Food? House?"*

"Yes! Food is in the house." I hoped he would be a good distraction so I could at least try and find the amulets.

"Food in house. Lots of food? Food in house." The goat seemed rather intrigued with the idea.

"Yes, make a lot of noise and we can try and get inside. You try over here, and I'll try from the otherside." Could goats do cooperative planning?

"Yes, food. Must scream." and with that the goat did in fact, start bleating and screaming to its little heart's content.

I hardly had time to move as I heard both the people inside wondering what the heck was going on. As fast as I could, I made my way around back and could hear them trying to shoo the goat away. Good luck with that. Goats do what they want.

Sadly, there was no back door. The small building did, thankfully, have a few open windows. Since they were lacking screens, I grabbed hold of the first ledge I came to and hauled myself up. I really needed to hit the gym more with James, but that was a problem for later. For now, it was time to search.

It was awkward sneaking into someone's bedroom, but I didn't have much else to work with. There were clothes everywhere in the small space, and to my delight, an amulet hanging off the doorknob. I quickly pocketed it and put the decoy on the door before slowly opening it.

No one was inside. I could hear them both outside still yelling for the goat to leave, and it sounded like it bit someone's shirt. They probably had it coming.

I glanced around the small living room slash kitchen slash dinning room setup. Nothing here stood out. Everything not being used was clean and put away. It didn't take much to guess that the Stepmomster probably ran a tight shift on that sort of thing, as long as it didn't directly involve her daughter.

With a sigh, I tried the next room over. It somehow reminded me of a china shop. I bet she would know if someone so much as stepped in there. Which I needed to do in order to even try and find the blasted thing. Carefully, I stepped in and felt magic ripple through me. She had more magic than I knew.

I could hear her yell, "someone's invaded!" and quickly dashed into the other room and out the window. I hustled to the side of the house, trying to decide if I wanted to hide in the woods or wait it out here.

"Get this goat out of the house!" Diamond screamed as I tried to catch my breath.

"Check your amulet." The Stepmomster at least had her priorities somewhat right.

After a moment I could hear her reply. "It's fine, right where I left it. I'm not Melanie, geeze."

"Just wear the thing. That way no one can take it."

"But it's uuugh-ley!" Diamond whined dramatically.

Ah, that's probably where the other one was. That Momster had it around her neck.

"Goat, can you get the chewy toy around the older crabby one's neck? I bet it's awesome." I listened carefully for the goat's thoughts, not entirely sure where he was anyway.

"Found food." the goat replied simply.

"The beast is eating our couch!" Diamond screamed. "Get out of here you nappy creature!"

Well, at least he was still causing a ruckus. This would be so much easier if Vincent were here.

Maybe not.

If she was wearing the amulet, the magic's enchantment was probably active, so being cloaked wouldn't help. Nadia would be the most ideal help.

A snarl caught my attention and I could hear a low growl coming from the woods. I tried to let my mind connect with whatever magical creature it was, hoping to convince it to leave me alone, but nothing came.

"Nadia?" I whispered loudly, hoping and wishing on every star possible it was her. Otherwise it was a magic made creature and I was pretty much fucked.

A red wolf head peered through the underbrush and I let out the breath I was holding.

"I've no idea how you got here, but I could use your help." I whispered as she approached.

Nadia sat up very still and waited. It would be so much easier if I could communicate with her, but since she wasn't actually an animal, I could not. Ash had no problems with it though. Her strange magic was always causing more questions to arise than answers could be found.

"The Stepmomster has the amulet. We need to retrieve it. My goat is distracting them, but you know, goats aren't that great at being helpful."

Nadia tilted her head to the side as if to say, 'oh really'.

"Yes, yes, I made a goat friend. We can get back to that later. I need you to grab that amulet first. She's got a lot of magic though." I explained, not sure what the best plan would be. "I don't think healing works here."

Nadia cocked her head to the side and whacked my leg with her paw. I tried to figure out what she was saying. "I don't know what else I can do. I don't have offensive magic; just healing, listening to animals, and oh. Wards. I can cover you from her magic. Duh. That's the plan then."

Nadia lowered her head as if agreeing.

"So I'll follow behind you-"

Nadia growled at me before I could finish the statement.

"I need to at least be able to see you." I replied firmly.

Nadia nodded her head in understanding.

"So, I guess I can climb a tree... Wait, I have a decoy amulet. If we stage it to look like it's dropped they'll leave you alone after a short distance."

Nadia gave a low growl.

"Is that a good growl or bad?"

She growled again.

"This would be easier if you were in human form." I sighed.

Nadia nodded but didn't shift.

"Are you stuck in that form?" I really hoped that wasn't the case, but she nodded back at me. Well, I guess everything wouldn't be easy, at least we could work together.

"Well, what path do you want to take? Do you want to hide the amulet along the path first?"

Nadia nodded, giving a happy almost bark. I pulled the decoy off from around my neck and handed it to her, and she took off. The second she returned, she motioned her head toward the trees.

"Time to hide then?" With her nod I carefully made my way into the trees, hoping no one inside saw me as I scaled one. Here went everything.

I tried to take comfort in the fact that Nadia actually knew and studied tactics in real life whereas all mine were gaming related. There was no resetting if this didn't work, and it was unlikely any second chances would come. So, I waited, magic at the ready.

Nadia crept to the open door and waited, lying low and ready to pounce. It took a few minutes but finally the goat ran out with Diamond and her mother chasing him away from the house. The two ran right past the door where Nadia was lurking.

Carefully, she stayed low as she followed behind them, waiting for them to stop. As soon as they did, she lunged and grabbed hold of everything along the back of the Stepmomsters neck. Both she and Diamond screamed as Nadia ripped loose the fabric before tackling her target to the ground. In a nanosecond she was off running, the amulet dangling from her mouth.

I set the ward behind her, concentrating hard to hold it steady.

Diamond was busy freaking out as her mother got to her feet, and threw out her hand. A dark wave of magic flashed out, striking my ward like a bolt of lightning, causing me to take in a sharp breath. It took more to keep the ward up and stable, but Nadia was gaining distance.

The Stepmomster cursed and went chasing after her, a frantic Diamond hot on her heels. I tried to track Nadia's magic and uphold the ward for as long as possible. After a while I lost sight and couldn't keep it up. I hoped she'd be fine. I did warn her I needed to see her, and she had done very well at vanishing into the woods.

After a few minutes I heard the two women making their way back through the woods. Both sounded angry, and were being overly loud, but they had no reason to know I was here.

"But why a wolf? Who would train a wolf to go after the amulet like that?" Diamond wondered.

"I don't know!" her mother replied angrily. "This whole thing is a mess, and if we don't hear from the others soon, we'll need to assume they were attacked as well."

"But we kept our magic weapons." Diamond said, as if she was so much better than the others.

"Indeed. We need to fortify the house now. No more leaving things open for wildlife or intruders to get in."

I watched them head inside, slamming the door behind them. In a short time I watched the open windows close one by one.

Minutes ticked by and I wondered at what point I should get down. It didn't feel safe now, but there might not ever be a time that it actually felt safe. Carefully, I scaled down the back of the tree and waited for a minute before continuing deeper into the woods. I didn't want to stay too close to the house, and I knew Nadia would have no trouble finding me.

That fact was made clear after a minute of walking when she appeared seemingly out of nowhere, necklace still in her teeth.

I carefully removed the amulet and pocketed it away. "Well, we did it. What next?"

Nadia bowed her head, not looking sure at all.

"Right. So, do we wait for instructions, try and listen in on the stepevils, or head toward the mountains like we had planned last night?" I wondered aloud.

Nadia gave a little huff and three small barks.

"Right, let's go and try and find our girls." I nodded, heading toward the mountains.

CHAPTER SIX

----Astrid----

You would think unicorns would be nicer, but they were all a bunch of low key trolls.

We followed them to another set of caves, with them ignoring just about all of our questions and commentary, while insisting breakfast was a must. I was delighted to see that food wasn't something purely unicorn feed, and involved plenty of fruits. Cat seemed to be taking in everything the best, while Arnessa was persistent in asking enough questions to start her own class on unicorns.

Finally, no one was eating and I couldn't take it any longer. "What did you even mean by my kind? What does that even mean?"

There was a lot of snickering. The unicorns were pleased as punch that I hadn't the slightest clue what they meant.

"When is your magic the strongest? When does it work best?" Arryn, the one who had been talking with us the most, replied.

I bit my lip as I considered the question. It was a good one. "Mostly when I feel strongly about something."

"Or?" The question was simple enough, the answer something I hadn't voiced but considered.

"It's not really when I desire it to work... more when it knows now is the time to work." I answered with a shrug, before leaning forward on the table, exchanging a look with my friends. They nodded knowingly.

"When has it worked outside of that?"

I was about to say 'never' when Nadia came to mind. There were a lot of weird moments early on, but they hadn't exactly made sense, or happened again. "I don't know... I've always been able to have books translate themselves. I guess in the last year I've noticed some magic has a song to it and I can use that song to help untangle the spell."

"Does all magic have a song?"

Why was this unicorn asking so many pointed questions? I sighed. "No."

"When does it?"

I looked back to Arnessa and Cat, the answer coming to mind, the pieces slowly clicking into place. "It's only happened with these weird Daeum situations, and I seem to be the only one to really hear it." I shook my head. "Just say it already."

Arnessa tilted her head. "What are you talking about?" She crossed her arms and leaned back in her chair.

"It should have been obvious before now." Cat tilted her head to the side. "But we all missed it."

Arnessa furrowed her brows at Cat before slowly nodding. "Oh."

I nodded as well. "It was right in front of our faces." I turned my attention to the unicorn. "So, what exactly is my title then? I know there are several types."

All eyes were on Arryn, our unicorn troll. There was a momentary pause and I was unsure if he was thinking of new questions or if he would outright tell me. *"Daeums are complicated beings. One cannot tell until your magic fully emerges, but once your magic emerges, you will either be able to learn more, or you will die here."*

"What does that mean?" Arnessa asked in horror.

"Either she's a good witch or a bad witch." Cat summed up, frowning at the unicorn.

I nodded. "Lesser Daeums aren't allowed. It was a Lesser Daeum that brought us here, and they probably figured if we did escape that you would keep us plenty busy."

"But why would they leave you in a place where you could die?" Arnessa looked my way.

"It's a choice that's out of their hands and into mine. With Nadia, she didn't have to fight the wolves. Here, I don't have to learn. To not know is to stay safe." I shrugged. "But who wouldn't want to know?"

Arryn knickered in amusement. *"And what do you choose?"*

"Clearly Lesser Daeums have escaped before, but that really doesn't matter in the long run. We've crossed paths with them too many times to not be on someone's watch list. Whatever happens, they'll be on me." I rambled for a moment, thinking aloud. If I was a Lesser Daeum then the good ones would find me in time unless I learned enough to hide and not be problematic. Was that an option? I assumed if I was a Noble I'd either be left alone or given more proper guidance. Decisions, decisions. "I'm really confused though. My parents were not Daeums." I let the question hang in the air unspoken.

The unicorn tilted his head. *"Standard or Lesser, Daeums are very tricky creatures. There is no telling exactly how things came to be, but I assure you, either you were given to your family or that one of your family members has a secret. What does it matter now? Are you ready to learn?"*

I doubted the unicorn had the true answer anyway so I sighed and turned to my friends before looking back at Arryn. "What about my friends?"

Arryn turned to glance their way. *"What about them? They are not Daeums. They have nothing new to learn from us. They will be returned home, with no memory of this place."*

"That isn't good enough." I said before either of them could speak up. "We were unwillingly brought here, and while I do appreciate your offer to teach me, I do *not* want their minds altered or messed with. Since it wasn't our fault, we should not be punished." I could feel the magic building around me, attaching itself with glee to the words I spoke.

Arryn didn't look bothered. *"You are completely capable of protecting them as you desire -if you take the chance to learn. I do not need to make such promises. I can keep my word, and you can complete your goal."*

The three of us looked at each other for a moment before Arnessa finally spoke, "Might as well try. It's the best option we have."

Cat nodded. "We only have our memories left to lose, but..." She hesitated. "I don't want anything bad happening to you, and there doesn't seem to be a way to protect you from their strong magic."

I weighed my options for a moment. "Learning would save us from future Daeum problems, and get us out of here with our memories." I turned my attention toward Arryn. "Where do I start?"

"This way." Arryn said as he led the way out of the room.

The three of us followed him, with the other unicorns going back to their own business. Arryn happily trotted through the maze of tunnels. It took no time for me to lose track of where we were going before we stopped in an empty chamber. It was dimly lit, only a few randomly glowing orbs to illuminate that otherwise dead end space.

Arryn quickly turned to face us, not wasting anymore time. *"The first lesson is to listen. All magic comes from the same source. The Daeum magic sings the loudest, but if they are all from the same source, they all have a song. Normal mortals cannot hear all of it. Doesn't matter. Heard or not, it is still there. Find me when you're done."*

We stared at him confused for the briefest of moments before his horn glowed amber and suddenly we were in a completely different cave. The light was equally dim, and there didn't appear to be an exit.

"What just happened?" Arnessa looked around. "Why did he move us?"

"I'm not sure he did." Cat looked around. "We don't know his magic, so it could be an illusion."

I nodded as I tried to reach out with my magic to find anything, but nothing was there. "I'm not exactly sure what to do here. I don't sense anything."

"Not to point out the obvious, but I'm sure that's the point." Cat chuckled a bit. "But I do have an idea."

We both glanced at her. "And that is?" Arnessa asked, genuinely curious.

"You know when magic gets super annoying and doesn't do the thing you want it to?" she asked, waiting for my nod before continuing. "Well, what is one thing you always feel?"

"Disappointment? Or are you talking magic wise?" I smirked before shrugging. "I don't know, it just ends abruptly."

"Does it end flat out or trail off?" Cat shrugged back at me.

Arnessa looked curiously at me. She didn't have difficulty with her magic and didn't really know the feeling. Cat was on to something though.

"It trails off, I let go because obviously that wasn't what we wanted and that thread is dead." I gave a small laugh. "Except it's really not."

"Exactly!" Cat agreed excitedly.

"I have no idea what you're both rambling about." Arnessa let out a sigh.

"Think of your magic, you pull certain threads right?" Cat asked her.

Arness nodded. "Yes, I pull from the power source, linking it with the magic inside me as I channel it into brews, or blanket it out into what I need it to be."

"Misfired magic is typically caused by pulling wrong. You pull from the power source, and then depending on the task, channel it with your inner magic. Sometimes, you just need to push it into things in general and not through your own magic. Like if you wanted to reheat your coffee."

Arnessa nodded slowly. "Magic is used, but since it's not going through you its signature is different and doesn't always work right. I can't light an actual fire, but yes, the basic magic of warming isn't difficult."

"So, Astrid is trying to search and channel through her inner magic." Cat summed up.

Arnessa caught on. "And that's not the point here."

I nodded. "I need to work with all the magic, and not just what's inside."

"That was a really roundabout way of getting to the point." Arnessa side eyed Cat who just shrugged.

"Never hurts to be thorough." Cat smiled before glancing at me. "So, what are you going to try now?"

I closed my eyes and reached out for the greater magic but all I did was try and feel it. After a minute or two of just letting it flow I noticed the faintest of hums. "I don't know, but there is something there."

"Try taking us just to the unicorns in general." Cat suggested, causing me to open my eyes and look at her.

"I don't know how." I wasn't sure what she was expecting there.

"Finding Arryn himself would be hard, but the unicorns have a unique signature. Find them, and pull the magic around us with our unique signatures. Then will our magical signatures to move to theirs" Cat explained.

"That is a really good idea." Arnessa agreed as she smiled at Cat. "You should teach classes on magical nonsense."

"Enchanting is nothing but having to think outside the box to make nonsense work." Cat shrugged, smiling proudly. "It'll be exhausting though, and I'm not sure how to protect against the drain."

Arnessa gave a small laugh. "That is rough but possible. Magic is about balance. It gives and takes, but maybe you'd be able to just redirect it?"

"Maybe." I bit my lip as I tried to consider things.

"Maybe not…" Cat trailed off as she paced the room. "What do we know about Daeums? They often appear as forces of nature. Forces of pure energy."

"Ah. So redirecting it would be more for a specific type of magical effect, but likely not this. Redirecting would be fantastic for illusions, for steering people away, or even manipulating memories." Arness continued on with Cat's line of thoughts.

"They may be able to just become one with all the magic and do whatever the heck they want." I mused.

"Why not? How else would one, just one, be able to change Nadia into an extreme being with locked magic, turn the entire staff into objects, hide the castle, manipulate global memories, impact information systems, create a barrier, the wolves, and like a dozen other things. It would be exhausting if they weren't able to just be one with it and channel it like they were part of magic itself." Cat pointed out.

"Like magic themselves huh?" I considered the idea briefly. "Guess I'll just have to try and find out then. Let's do this."

There wasn't much to lose, everything was very low stakes at the moment at least. Truth be told, I'd rather deal with trolling unicorns than a Lesser Daeum.

I reached out for the magic once more, letting it cover me. The reason you weren't supposed to let magic just course through you was because it could overwhelm and kill you. It normally just knocked people out though, since most lost hold of it when it shocked their system. I knew I had to be careful, but just how carefully did I have to approach this?

A small stream of power was within my grasp and I let out a breath as I went against my upbringing. The bit of power was very tingly, and while it didn't hurt, it felt like I had drank the coffee equivalent of a lightning bolt. Aside from that, everything felt normal.

I tried to keep my mind on track as I reached out for more magic, followed along not just by a thread of power but the entire blanket, trying to search nearby for the unicorns.

Nothing magical was close.

I could feel the difference in power Arnessa and Cat were giving off, but as I stretched out for miles, and miles, nothing else stood out.

It clicked that it shouldn't. Unicorns didn't want to be found. In fact, when we first met them, they felt more like the core of the planet. With that in mind I let a bit of the magic go, looking instead for that power they were originally giving off.

Cat was right. I couldn't pick Arryn out of the bunch but I could find a large group of them. That would be enough for now. With that location firmly in my grasp, I wrapped the magic coursing through me around the three of us and shifted it to be next to the unicorn magic.

I let out a huge breath as I sunk to the ground in our new location, the magic leaving me far too fast. I hadn't even realized when we moved that I let go.

"You did it!" Arnessa laughed excitedly.

Cat patted my back. "I wasn't expecting it to work so fast. Way to go."

I nodded, catching my breath as the unicorns watched us with curious glances. When I felt well enough, I stood back up. "Well, that was something."

"Now where did Arryn go off to?" Cat mused, glancing around.

Arnessa glanced around. "He's not in this room. I think I might have found his trail though." She shrugged.

"Lead on." I nodded toward her. "He just said find him, he didn't say which of us had to."

The three of us smiled widely. I wondered what the next 'lesson' would be.

CHAPTER SEVEN

----Vincent----

After an hour of wandering after I grabbed the sword, I gave up and found a nice, quiet, deadend to curl up and hide in, locking myself in a thick illusion that would take a Daeum themself to unravel. Something I knew Melanie wasn't capable of. Her ice magic might be problematic if I ran into her, but that wouldn't be the end of the world. Our different destruction magics were on the same level, and she had nothing extra to help her. I had my illusions.

For the first time in my life that wasn't actually comforting.

We both had the same help. There was a Daeum on our side, and she was just shifting us around, giving us tasks. It was very helpful to be in the right place, but what if the other one noticed? What if the evil Daeum found out and just shifted us back? Or worse? No one had actually said what would happen if one or both of them got fed up. These beings were too overpowered, even for those of us considered strong.

I tried to shake off the dread as I got up. I needed to think clearly if I wanted to get out of here. I briefly wondered if this was the maze we were eventually supposed to end up in. The illusion magic was hard to find, but once I found the correct path and disrupted the thread I was able to finally leave the tunnel. It felt like someone had already taken it apart and fixed it, leaving the threads more jagged than they should be. I wasn't about to complain. One less problem for me, and I was more than happy to finally be out of that dark mess of tunnels.

It was closer to noon now from the way the sun hung in the sky.

"Now what?" I asked myself as I took in the greenery in the distance.

I had completed my task, and thankfully it wasn't even hard. The sword hung loosely at my side, its ability making me uneasy. I hoped Cat could remove the enchantment, or maybe there was a way to destroy it. No one needed a weapon of this caliber.

"You need to come with me now." a voice said, causing me to look around.

No one was there.

I carefully scrutinized the area once before repeating with magic, letting it scan for everything. Illusions were all over this area. From the density of the forest, even to some of the rocks, it was difficult to see what wasn't made of magic. Several of the spells were much stronger than anything I could do, but very different from the magic I had felt with the Daeum.

There was no other statement to help me pinpoint who had spoken. "I'm listening, but I clearly cannot hope to follow if you're invisible." I replied, making no commitments to actually follow along.

There was a chuckle, but it sounded off, almost like a horse was mocking me.

"If I appear before you, I'll have to erase your memory. Instead, I have a friend who will show you where to go."

A holographic unicorn appeared a few yards in front of me. As far as unusual things went, this actually felt fairly underwhelming. Truthfully, it was nice compared to being sent into the void before being dropped into a cave.

"Follow. Your friends need you."

I wished that surprised me. Since the Daeum hadn't given me any additional guidance, I had nothing to lose by following random mythical ponies around. "Do I at least get to know what I'm going into?"

"He's following them."

That made enough sense. The crazed tracker was making our life hell. "Donny?" I asked anyway as I walked toward the waiting hologram.

"We know not his name, just that he's touched with her magic. She will be eliminated once we find her."

Yep, that had to be Donny.

The unicorn hologram started to move and I had to walk quickly in order to keep up with it. I doubted I had much time to complain about the fast pace. If Donny was on anyone's trail, he had those arrows. They never missed. If someone wasn't expecting them...

I let the thought drift off and hoped I wouldn't have to worry about it. Instead, I focused on keeping the unicorn in my sight and avoiding tripping over anything.

"You should hide now. I won't lose track of you."

I didn't doubt it. Whoever was leading me on this chase was far stronger than me. Without further prompting, I called my magic around me, willing myself to blend in with my surroundings. I let my footsteps be muffled, even made it look as if the wind was passing through the space I occupied. This would be tiring, but I had plenty of time before I needed to lower the level of the illusion. It should be more than enough to cause Donny grief.

We seemed to travel for ages, the hologram unicorn easily navigating the terrain like the illusion it was. I was starting to get tired when it abruptly stopped.

"Just ahead." it declared before vanishing.

I blinked in surprise. I wasn't sure what I was expecting, but that abrupt end was not it. With a deep breath, I continued on, much more carefully now. At first there seemed to be nothing, and that's when it clicked that there really was nothing. No bird song, no signs of wild life whatsoever.

Then I saw him, the asshole whose picture I had memorised on the first night.

Freaking Donny was slowly making his way through the woods. Something about the magic around him felt off, tainted. He appeared to be tracking someone, maybe something. Whatever he was doing, I was going to make a mess of it.

----Nadia----

What a mess we had gotten ourselves into. At least I had the upper hand as far as information went. Our biggest problem was me being stuck in my wolf form, and the man who could talk to animals couldn't understand me. Being shifted into a wolf form did not in fact make me a wolf. Still, I had some good information and was pleased to know that we were in fact working our way to take down a Lesser Daeum.

I had awoke this morning and had gotten ready in record time when a bright light overtook me. "Blasted Daeum." I had cursed loudly, and only slightly unjustly. I didn't know the intent, but one could not blame me for being permanently tired of them.

"We meet once more, but under very different terms." If the voice didn't give her away, that line certainly did. What a way to reintroduce yourself.

"What is it that you want now?" I replied, not caring that every ounce of exasperation showed. "I thought you would leave me alone by now?"

"It is a complicated matter. While I never intended to come to you in this way again, we need each other's help." '

That had my full attention, mental attention anyway. What could an all powerful being possibly need help with? Too bad I still couldn't see her. The light was blinding and I had my eyes otherwise covered. "I am listening and open to what you may have to say."

She gave a small laugh. "You see, your beloved Astrid is very unique. I had laid low to watch her magical growth and see if there was a time appropriate to show her more. Then a Lesser of my kind decided it was safe to meddle, believing I was gone. She won't hold her end of the bargain with the fools who summoned her. In fact, she'll kill your Astrid to harvest her magic. First she just needed someone else to collect the right things for her."

"And that imbecile was more than willing to do so because he assumed she would just help." I clicked my tongue. "Not everyone holds to their promises. I'm only lucky you did."

The Daeum huffed. "A noble being always stays true to the course."

"And it was luck they they summoned a Noble one. The council was fools, though not nearly as much as this Donny fellow. What a disaster." I took a breath and exhaled slowly. "What do you need, and how can this help us?"

"I need to lie low. I want this Lesser to fully emerge so I can strike her down." The coldness of her words sent a shiver down my spine. "But I do not have any desire to see harm come to your group. So, we'll start by removing the tools the Lesser has given the mortals."

I nodded. It was a reasonable plan. "What of Astrid and the others? Are they safe?"

"Perfectly so. I spoke with another friend who is going to help them. They are fine for the moment. Your other friend however, this Rey fellow, he needs help."

I frowned. "What does he need help with?" The realization caught up with me a moment later than it should have. "He should still be here! What did you do?"

"He is trading out amulets."

I had to accept that was going to be my only answer for now. "Fine. I'll help him succeed."

"There is a catch." Her words came out slowly.

"There always is." I wasn't surprised, and stated it as a fact. "What is the catch?"

"If I move you, since I've already left a magical impression on you once before, the Lesser will be on to me. However, if I temporarily force you into one of your forms, the impression won't stick."

There were worse things. Honestly, as long as I never had to retake that beast form again I would be fine. "Very well, we'll make it work. Send me as the wolf."

"You don't wish to know how long it'll last?" She sounded surprised.

"Whatever I must do to save the others and stop this madness." I replied, not afraid to make this commitment. It would eventually come to an end, and if this Daeum wanted to destroy the Lesser, my bet was on sooner rather than later.

"When you find Astrid, she can ease you back." I felt a rush of magic as her words ended before the intensity of light vanished, leaving me in the woods.

I wasn't sure which woods, or where I was. Everything smelled unusual, this place had animals I hadn't encountered before, but I could faintly pick up on Rey's scent. That was all I needed, and the most important fact, so off I went.

After meeting up with Rey, and managing to switch the amulets, we were at a loss on what to do next. Being stuck in wolf form, there was little I could actively add to the conversation. At least Rey was clever enough to understand the overall mission of what we needed to do without words. We completed the amulet quest, now we had to find the others.

That didn't change how much I absolutely hated my words and intentions being guessed at. The only positive thing was that my companion thought highly of me and wasn't trying to put negative words in my mouth. Rey did his best to ask yes or no questions so I could actively respond the way I wanted to. More or less.

"I feel like we've got to be close to something." Rey said as he paused. The trees were getting taller here, the mountains harder to see through the dense canopy of leaves. "Should we keep going straight?"

I glanced around at all the greenery, taking in as much as I could, and looking for any signs of a reasonable trail. Nothing stood out. This place wasn't touched by anything other than the wildlife that lived here. I gave a vague nod before moving forward a bit more and pausing, something catching my nose.

Rey stopped immediately with me. "Is this a good thing?"

The scent was familiar but not one I could immediately identify. I shook my head no. If I couldn't figure it out, it was best to be leery.

Rey nodded as he looked around. "The animals aren't acting weird or saying anything strange, so that much is good. Is it a sound?" He waited for me to respond before continuing on with smell, which I agreed with.

"A bad smell..." he mused. "You know all of us. Maybe it's one of the others we're supposed to be avoiding. Is it one of the two we grabbed the amulets from?"

I liked that he kept on track with this. I shook my head. It wasn't them.

"So, that leaves Melanie and Donny." Rey raised an eyebrow. "Either of those?"

I wasn't positive. It felt familiar but also, not. I hadn't met Melanie before though so I gave a slow nod. Maybe it was Donny, but it felt like it wasn't at the same time. Magic be damned.

Rey lowered his voice. "Eastward the animals are much quieter. Someone is in that direction. If it's Melanie with the sword we need to be really careful."

I shook my head, hoping he'd understand.

"Don't think it's her?" Rey asked and I gave a slow nod. "If it's Donny, we need to stay out of sight. Damn OP bow."

It was too overpowered of a gift. I wondered how they got so many things. I couldn't even guess the cost. I doubted that the Lesser Daeum gave them up freely.

Rey's voice dropped low. "I'm not entirely sure how it works, this bow thing. If he's aiming at me can it go through a visible ward? Or if he can see the ward would it hit the ward because that is part of a visible target?" He glanced down at me and shrugged. "Sorry, I don't expect an answer, and I don't really think a ward would actually be enough."

I didn't either, so I nodded. It was unlikely the target would be the ward, even if Donny could see it. He was desperate and straight to the point. If he wanted to shoot either of us, he would think and aim directly for us.

A thought occurred to me. If we were being followed by Donny, our best bet was to remove the bow before he could use it. If we snuck up on him, we could certainly do that. A plan slowly formed in my mind.

With a gruffy low growl, I trotted forward, causing Rey to move faster to keep up. I put a fair distance between us and that strange scent when I started to look for the perfect tree. Once I found it, I growled at it, looking from Rey to it, hoping he'd get the idea.

"I'm getting the idea you have a plan," he whispered. "But why do you want me trapped in a tree? If he finds me, I'm basically screwed."

I gave a slow nod. That was exactly the point. I moved to hide into the bush across the way, so in theory Donny's back would be toward me, before poking my head out.

Rey stared at me for a moment. "So, you ambush him? I can't climb out of the tree fast enough to help after that."

At least he knew his weakness but I couldn't think of a better plan at the moment, and time was running low. We could walk for days, but that jerk would easily tail us.

Rey sighed. "Well, I guess here it goes." He reached up and pulled himself into the tree, quickly ascending and moving branches to better cover himself.

I hated to risk him like this, but it was our best bet. Donny was likely tracking the footprints more than my own markings. I had seen similar enough ones everywhere so I was not the only large wolf here. I rarely was; many of my kind loved the freedom woods gave us.

I made a point to leave a few different trails heading off before resettling into my hiding spot and waiting.

And waiting.

And waiting.

Donny took his time approaching us. He likely realized we were on to him and wanted more of an advantage. It's harder to hit a knowing target, but not by much with a magical bow. I doubted that he cared. It wasn't fair. It lacked sportsmanship. Donny likely saw it as something he had earned, something he rightly deserved in order to get what he wanted. Every story Ash told me about him only solidified that thought. Oh how I loathed him.

If he thought I'd let him lay a single finger on her he had another thing coming.

My inner wolf almost vibrated with anger and fury barely restrained by my human side. Ash wouldn't be happy to hear I literally ripped him apart. She would prefer a less gory route. At this point I could push for his powers stripped. With three royals against him it could easily be done. That would be satisfying enough. Even if there were less screams.

Donny approached the tree Rey was hidden in and smirked. I knew he couldn't see Rey, even I couldn't anymore. Still, Donny had a smug look on his face, his tracking magic leading him to exactly the point where Rey's feet left the ground.

"You're trapped, but I'll be a man of honor if you help me out." Donny laughed, its dark tone seeming to echo more than what was natural.

Rey, of course, did not reply.

After a few moments Donny clicked his tongue disapprovingly before chuckling. "You think you stand a chance of beating me? I've got better weapons, skills, and looks. There is nothing you can hope to beat me with."

I would have gagged if I were human. This trash panda really thought he was the best thing since sliced bread. The arrogance seeped out of him like a virus, the noxious bacteria of his existence ready to latch on and destroy all that was good.

Again, Rey did not respond. I couldn't even hear him. My eyes narrowed where I saw him vanish.

Oh, he was good.

Donny, however, was oblivious as he continued to talk to the tree. "You see, this bow I got right here will hit you. No magic can stop it, but if you agree to work with me, I won't kill you. Nothing is getting in my way this time."

He held the bow up in the air, as if to show it off before letting his arm drop. As Donny continued to prattle on about how his plan was the best and Rey would come to understand, I watched Donny's hand. His grasp quickly laxed.

I lunged after it, loving the perfection of the moment.

Surprise was on my side and by the time Donny realized it was out of his grasp, I was already off running. Did it matter where? Not to me! I pushed myself to go as far back the way we had come before looping and zagging around, knowing his tracking magic could follow me, but goodness! was it going to be a nightmare of a path.

I was shocked when something suddenly appeared in my path, causing me to slam into it. Stunned, I lay on the ground a moment, spots dancing before my eyes as I heard someone laugh darkly.

The sultry sweet laugh rang in my ears for a moment as the voice registered. It was that young brat from the cabin. Where did she come from?

"Mother! I found that wolf." the girl called out.

My vision was coming back and I was able to shake my head. I forced myself up as The girl, likely Diamond, walked away calling for her mom again. Everything ached and I realized I didn't know what magic these two had. A woman appeared in the distance, a black oozing magic snaking its way to me.

I tried to make a run for it, but it caught up and slid up my leg before snaking around my neck as it pulled me to the ground. It held my throat firmly in place, making it impossible for me to get back up and run. What was this magic? The darkness was vile and unlike anything I had experienced before.

Diamond cackled, clapping her hands gleefully as they approached. "That was fun! Now what do we get to do with the little beast?"

"Hmm... I've got an idea" Her mother's voice sounded low, dark, and like every cliche horror movie murderess.

I tried to summon every bit of magic I had within me to break from this form. The binding wouldn't budge.

A large snap that sounded like a full grown tree collapsing sounded from behind us.

"What was that?" I heard Diamond ask, a quiver of fear in her voice.

A wave of magic washed over me. It's power comforting and familiar. I stopped resisting, hoping beyond a doubt that Vincent's magic would be enough to keep me safe. Struggling hadn't done me an ounce of good so far.

"Where did the beast go?" Diamond's mother snarled. "I feel my magic on it."

"And it moved with it?" Diamond sounded confused. "Totes weird. What sort of wolf can do that?"

There was a pause as the sound of another cracking tree came nearer.

"What is going on?" Diamond moved away from me and the sound.

Another moment passed before her mother finally replied. "I don't know. It feels weird. Too strong." She started walking away, the magic dropping.

It took everything in me not to take a deep breath, the air coming more easily to my lungs now that I wasn't pinned.

"Where are we going?" Diamond asked. I watched her look around frantically.

"That spell was supposed to hold my target in place. Clearly, it only stayed with the creature. We need to reconfigure our plans." she replied.

There was another loud snapping sound causing them both to stop, barely within earshot.

"I don't see another. Is it an illusion?" Diamond asked, fear sticking to every syllable.

"Don't be an idiot. The amulets would show it." Her mother rubbed her necklace lovingly. "That Daeum proved that to us several times over. These woods are trouble. Nothing more than nasty magic." She turned on heel, Diamond following closely behind.

I stayed motionless as I waited for Vincent. I wasn't sure if the magic was just on this spot or on me in general and did not want to disrupt his work.

Finally Rey appeared in the distance with Vincent at his side. The two men looked tired, but other than gross and sweaty, they appeared completely fine. They lifted the spell from me and I was relieved that no more trouble seemed to be afoot.

I went to meet them but paused, turning back around. The fools had left the bow. It was wooden, blending in nicely with the roots of the tree it landed by. I grabbed it in my mouth and trotted to the guys.

Mission accomplished.

CHAPTER EIGHT

----Cat----

Looking for Arryn was like finding a needle in a haystack. All the magic felt just a little different, the unicorns having their own variations in primary talents like the rest of us, but trying to track a single one just brought things back to that earthy, core, feel. If that made any sense. Logic as we knew it didn't apply here. Somehow Ash, despite seeming to be human, was not.

She seemed to be ignoring that fact and only honing in on the extra magic. I couldn't blame her. I wasn't sure I would react any differently. Figure out the magic, set things right, and GTFO as soon as physically possible.

It occured to me that we could actually all leave now. Ash just needed to focus on home, but I didn't blame her for wanting to learn more. We would need all the extra talent possible to get this Lesser Daeum to leave us the heck alone. At least the unicorns also hated her. She couldn't easily bother us here with the stabby trolls ready to shank a deity.

"I think we're doing this wrong." I said after we had been searching for what felt like much too long.

Arnessa and Ash stopped and looked back at me.

"I'm more than happy to hear new ideas." Arnessa agreed, sounding tired. "Their magic is becoming more tangled the more I try and figure it out."

"Same honestly." Ash replied.

"So, I don't know what you felt when you met them, but they feel like they've been here since stardust. Like they are as much of the planet as the rocks and soil we walk on." I explained, trying to put what I was feeling to words.

Ash slowly nodded her head. "But how can we use that to our advantage?"

Arnessa shrugged. "Locating the right strand in magic is usually how we find things. Here, it gets more tangled. I can't even think of an opposite way of doing that."

"Maybe it's not the opposite way? If it comes from the planet itself forming, it's rooted differently than our evolution and magic." I gave a shrug not really having an answer.

"If they were here from the beginning…" Ash mused. "Let's think of them as the same stardust making the planet. Magical stardust. What if they are so closely connected to that they are both here and not here at the same time? That they can just become one with the land around them, break down into the most basic of atoms, and travel through both magic and their physical form."

"By going with that theory, if we can't find Arryn, he might not actually be present and we just need to call his form to us." It wasn't the weirdest thing, I just wasn't expecting to think sciencey since enchanting classes.

Arnessa nodded. "Actually, that makes a lot of sense. Things would get so tangled magically trying to find them because they can be anywhere in a blink, so they are nowhere and everywhere at once."

"I doubt we have the magic to call him." I nodded at Arnessa before turning to Ash. "But you can. So call a troll and let's start the next step."

Ash smirked. "Why not try?" She closed her eyes, and for a moment I felt nothing before a very similar feeling with her magic as I did with the unicorns.

Then Arryn was in front of us.

"That took less time than normal." The unicorn sounded rather pleased. *"I barely had time to finish a task for a friend. Look at you. About time someone kept me busy."*

I wasn't sure if this was a good thing or not, but hey, we did it! Ash really did it, but still. Group effort developing the ideas. I wish I could have implemented some of it.

"What task?" Arnessa asked curiously.

"Lead a mage to a hunter." The unicorn laughed, full on whinny-ing.

"I don't know what I was expecting." Arnessa sighed.

Ash shrugged. "So, what's next Arryn? How can we get this Lesser Daeum to leave us alone?"

Arryn tilted his head to the side for a moment. *"We should meet my friend."*

He started to trot off, not bothering to see if we'd follow.

I bit my lip as I followed behind, Arnessa at my side and Ash a step further behind us. This felt random, but at the same time, maybe not. We were missing a lot of information.

"What friend is this?" I finally asked.

Arryn didn't reply at first. *"Her name is hers to give. She has a particular problem with this Lesser being. More than normal. She wants to destroy her."*

Well now, that was information I could get behind. "And she wants our help? Or what?"

The silence stretched on as we waited, traveling endlessly through the tunnels that probably magically did have no end, and waited for Arryn to finally reply.

"Help is an interesting word. She might word it that way."

We glanced at each other, not liking that.

"And what does she actually want?" Arnessa asked for us.

"Bait."

Ah. Well, there were only so many ways to lure a Daeum out, and if we were hanging out with unicorns, she wasn't going to readily show herself again.

"Better than a sacrifice." It was true.

"It's like our last D&D campaign." Arnessa gave a small laugh.

"I do *not* want to play bait to a deity." Ash sighed. "But how else do we lure her out? If we take her down, Donny and the trash bandits have nothing going for them. It solves everything."

"It really does." Arnessa agreed.

"But we're going to need one heck of a plan to get out of this one." I added, remembering how terribly that particular campaign ended.

"This friend we're going to see, Arryn." Ash stated hesitantly, "If she wants the Lesser gone, does that make her a Daeum as well?"

There weren't many other options. Not that I knew of anyway.

Arryn gave a slight nod. *"She is."*

Something about his answers was bothering me. He was normally more... amused and troll-y. Here he was very serious. Was he concerned about where this was going?

Something felt off, and before the thought of off-ness could register everything around us went black. Suddenly we were in a warm field, the mountains in the distance now. A power radiated strongly behind me, causing me to turn only to see a blinding light. Darn deities and their magic.

----Arnessa----

Blinding lights were too much theatrics for me. It reminded me in too many ways of how my step mother would rattle things, cause all sorts of inconveniences before striking down an inevitable punishment, and then blame me for the mess.

I crossed my arms, and turned away from the light, not interested in playing this game. If they wanted a face to face talk either they could assume a more tolerable form, or I'd face away. That seemed to be fair. Why cause yourself a headache by talking and staring into the sun?

Thankfully, the light seemed to dim some, and I turned, seeing the being was still far too bright to look at but this was at least less obnoxious.

"Can we do this meeting without the brightness?" Ash asked bluntly. At least all of our thoughts were on the same page.

An angelic voice gave a small laugh before replying, "If I do that, you'll be most disappointed."

That wasn't the answer I was expecting. Maybe more 'I'm too scary for you' or 'my true form can never be known!' but instead she thought we'd be dissapointed. Well then.

"I am actually all for disappointment right about now," Cat said. "Something more normal sounds wonderful."

"Agreed," I chimed in without thinking.

We were asking a Deity to chill. This could bite us pretty hard if we weren't careful.

She gave a small laugh. "On one condition."

"What would that be?" Ash asked hesitantly.

"You learn the path."

Ash didn't even hesitate. "Only if Nadia is included."

I looked over at Cat who shrugged. It was a fair enough request. At least in my mind.

The moment stretched on uncomfortably before the Daeum gave a small laugh. "All your friends may be included, if they never speak of what is learned in this place. The unicorns prefer to be unknown."

I snorted. They had been more than clear on that point.

"What's the price of us being able to know all this?" I asked, not wanting to be surprised later.

No pause from the Daeum this time. "You will always be a target for the Lessers. They like to remove threats so they can cause mayhem. Memories or mayhem? That is what you must decide."

"Could be worse." Cat replied. "I've made up my mind."

Ash nodded as well. "As have I."

Great. I was the only one wanting to think over my options today. I had another question before I could rightfully decide. "There's no guarantee they'll leave us be, even without the memories, is there?"

"There are never guarantees with chaotic forces." the Daeum replied simply.

Of course there wasn't. I'd rather keep my memories intact. It had been my goal since the beginning, and it wasn't about to change now. I just wanted to know all my options. "I've decided then."

The brightness faded from view, and wow was she right about the disappointment.

"Elora?" Ash asked with as much confusion as I felt.

She gave a small wave.

"What in the heck?" I frowned.

Elora was another Noble. Her family was rather quiet and usually little was heard of them or their country. They attended events, but weren't the best dressed, or most out there. They were simple, always neutral, always middle of the road.

Cat crossed her arms. "When you said we'd meet again soon, I expected it was some event I had forgotten about. You've got a lot of explaining to do."

Elora shrugged. "Do I? It makes a lot of sense. How would a divine being be able to hear things on this little planet out of everywhere in the universe? Unless I happened to reside here. We are very powerful, but I wouldn't say entirely omniscient."

The snarky brat. I shook my head. "Okay, that does explain a bit, but why live here if you could literally live anywhere?" This could not be the most exciting planet, though apparently we were hiding unicorns.

Elora gave another shrug. "I was born here. Daeums live a long time, but we don't exactly live forever. Several hundred years, give or take. It's custom to visit neighboring systems and realms at about a hundred, but I've got a ways to go before that."

There were so many things I wanted to ask, but now didn't seem like the right moment. "I don't feel like we have time for this right now." I sighed.

Ash gave a sigh as well. "We probably don't. What's the plan, and what's going on with the people we care about? There's no way they haven't gotten involved."

"Oh, they're fine." Elora smirked. "Arryn helped out a bit. I had your people grab those annoying weapons. We just need to rendezvous with them, but first a plan. If those three are left alone for a bit, causing some trouble, that keeps the focus away from you. I still have my magic watching them."

I hated that she was probably right. The other Daeum would be trying to figure out what was going on there since we were with the unicorns. Hopefully that would buy us the time we needed in order to set something in motion.

"What's your idea?" I asked.

Elora winked, a menacing look spreading across her normally carefree face. "Here's what I'm thinking…"

CHAPTER NINE

----Rey----

I was pretty certain I never wanted to be in the woods again. I had too many weird prickler things sticking to me, stabbing into my skin, leaves kept getting caught in my hair, and I was fairly certain the same three bugs kept landing on me. I just wanted to find everyone, get home, and shower until the hot water ran out.

But I tried not to outwardly complain.

The second Nadia ran off with the Donny's bow, I was safe to get down. It was much harder than I anticipated since I moved over a few trees. The bigger branches made changing trees and hiding in the greenery easy. Donny lost the trail the second I was off the ground. The idiot really thought he could catch up to Nadia, or maybe just track her down. Either way, I was on the ground, free, and I wasn't sure what to do now.

I tried to concentrate, see if I could figure out where Nadia was going, but I was never all that talented with that. I could listen to the animals, but they cared most about their immediate area, making it hard to figure out where Nadia went after a short span. With a sigh, I decided it was probably best to just stay put and let her find me. Nadia could sniff me out, and it was the most sensible plan. The best we could do with the inability to communicate normally.

I felt a shift in magic and turned to my left, laughing. "Where did you come from?" I asked Vincent as he seemingly appeared out of nowhere.

"I'd say you're never going to believe it, but heavens be damned I could believe anything right about now." He shook his head as he reached me. "I don't know who exactly led me here, but I followed a holographic unicorn."

"That is weirder than normal." I shrugged, mildly impressed by the randomness of it all, but we needed to stay focused. "Think you can find Nadia?"

"I'm guessing that was her who took off as a wolf." Vincent waited for my nod before continuing, "Yeah, I can try."

He concentrated, closing his eyes as he searched magically. After a while he finally spoke, "She is moving stupid fast. It won't help to find her until she slows or stops."

I nodded and realized he couldn't see that with his eyes closed. "Sounds fair. She's got to be feeling tired. We've done nothing but run and travel."

Vincent opened his eyes. "Mine's been less exciting, but also eventful." He patted the sword at his side before launching into his side of events. After I filled him in on the bit that happened with us, he looked for Nadia again. "She's stopped. It looks like she was looping back around. I wonder why she paused. Not terribly far but..."

Vincent set off at a run and I was right behind him. I could feel his magic quickly draping over us, our steps going silent as we otherwise crashed through the underbrush. I assumed the worst while I tried to hope for the best.

We ducked and weaved through the woods until he came to a halt. I was several steps behind him, exhaustion starting to win out. That's when I heard them. I turned in the direction of their voices and found Nadia. The Stepmomster and her delightful spawn were at it again with the mayhem.

Vincent waved for me to hold up. At this point I was fine with him having a plan. I wasn't sure what I could do aside from try and ward off magic and heal everyone later. Vincent concentrated hard for several moments before a thunderous snapping sound happened behind the group we were watching. The ground shook and a mixture of dust and leaves went up as if a tree had fallen. The noise surprised the Stepmomster and Diamond, causing concern for the older and the perfect amount of fear in the younger.

I watched Vincent masterfully work his magic, causing fake destruction and hiding Nadia until finally causing them to take off. We watched them walk off, suddenly vanishing into a black void.

Because that wasn't ridiculously villainesque.

Assuming it was as safe as it could be, Vincent dropped the magic. We met in the middle, Nadia with the bow, Vincent with the sword, and I had both amulets.

"Well, that was a morning." I yawned, ready to be done with this entire month. Nadia dropped the bow at our feet.

We all exchanged an exhausted and defeated look.

Nadia gave a tired snarl before flopping to the ground. There was no way to hashtag mood this moment so I just sat down beside her, Vincent joining us.

"I've no idea where to go next." Vincent shook his head as he yawned.

I gave a slow nod, pointing vaguely from where we'd come from. "The place that the double stepmonster menaces were staying at is over there."

Vincent motioned toward the mountains. "Melanie was hauled up that way by the mountains."

Nadia just grunted tiredly, kicking the bow aside so she could get more comfortable.

I yawned. "I wasn't expecting to feel this wiped from so little. Sure we traveled, but I got a good night's sleep."

Vincent shrugged. "I sort of did. Took a power nap in a cave. Used some illusions to keep everyone who might wander by away." He yawned loudly, cutting off anything else he was going to say.

Nadia sat up looking at us, confused, as we both started to yawn more. She gave a growl that I just couldn't make sense of. My brain refused to operate correctly, a thick unexplained exhaustion settling in. I felt like I should ask her something, but words didn't come as my eyes refused to stay open, my head becoming too heavy to keep up.

Nadia knocked into me before tugging on the sword at Vincent's belt. She growled over and over before moving to me, snagging the amulets, and dragging them away. A moment later she was back trying to tug at the sword.

My head no longer felt leaden and I watched her confused. Why had she removed the- oh. I was awake now and before I wasn't. Something was very wrong here, which was obvious now that the random punishing sleep spell was gone.

Vincent had already slumped over, asleep, and I sighed. "Let me try." I said to Nadia and managed to get the sword off, casting it aside with a small throw.

"I don't know how you figured that out." I yawned the last bit of tiredness away, as I stretched out and forced myself to my feet.

Nadia huffed before nudging Vincent. After a few less than nice shakes, Vincent yawned and sat up confused.

"Welcome back." A smirk spread across my face.

"What just happened?" He asked, looking around as if he had the worst, most disorienting nap of his life.

"I don't know how Nadia figured out what was wrong, but those things we grabbed from team bad guy put us to sleep." I summed up with the limited understanding I had.

Nadia gave a growl and started to walk away from us.

I called to her, "Are we supposed to follow?"

Nadia barked in reply.

Vincent rubbed his eyes. "But what about these stupid things? We should take them right? But then we're screwed aren't we?"

"I don't know. We each had them for a while, so maybe it's time based? Or that Daeum decided to use them against us. I don't even know if I care anymore." I raked my hand through my hair.

Nadia gave a low growl before trotting up to Vincent and nudging him.

"I don't know what you want." He sighed, frustration evident in his voice.

"Let's break it down then." I suggested, crossing my arms. "We need to follow you, but we need to do something about the weapons. Do you want us to bring them?"

Nadia shook her head.

"Do you want us to hide them?" I tried.

Nadia nodded before bumping into Vincent.

"Use your master level voodoo and let's see where we're going." I instructed Vincent.

"I have no idea how you figured all of that out." He closed his eyes. A moment later the objects vanished from sight.

"I know this is going to surprise you, but I don't just play video games. I also play board and card games, and grew up with charades." It helped I was used to the limited ways animals could communicate, but really it was more likely thanks to charades.

Vincent laughed as Nadia took the lead again. This adventure was an unending battle of weirdness that rivaled some of our D&D campaigns. Without another word, Vincent cloaked us in magic as we followed behind Nadia.

I was beyond fazed with the current developments, wondering what sort of annoying novel I had gotten myself sucked into. Aside from the momentary confusion, Vincent was looking equally unsurprised. I didn't want to know what could come our way next.

Not wanting to know didn't stop the inevitable as we suddenly fell into a pit. We hadn't fallen completely to the ground, just long enough to be surprised and whisked away into a dark void, only for the light to suddenly return as we landed hard on a cave floor. The random location change felt like a whiplash and left me momentarily short of breath.

"Now, who are you trouble makers?" A sultry voice came from the darkness deeper in the cave.

Nadia was on her feet first, growling. Anger and fury radiated from her being as she snapped her teeth toward this mystery person.

"I've no use for you." the voice said before a wave of magic cast Nadia into the wall hard, knocking her out. A tall cloaked figure stepped into the faint light, only her dark blood red lips visible. "You two hardly look useful, but bait is always fun." She chuckled darkly.

Vincent instantly went to try and cast something at her, but she waved it off before throwing out a hand. I was ready with a ward, only for it to not matter. It shattered like glass, the spell coming through full force, throwing us back into the wall.

Dark spots danced before my eyes as I tried, but failed, to regain any footing.

"Now, now, no need for that." A small laugh escaped her lips before everything went cold and dark.

----Astrid----

Normally when someone said they had a plan, I was a bit skeptical. An array of half planned thoughts was not a plan. Elora did in fact have a full fledged plan. The different threads you guessed at and the actions for each reaction that she had already planned out was amazing. She knew exactly what she was doing, and made everything very easy to follow along with.

I hated it.

There was not a single aspect where everyone came out unscathed. The first part of her plan was already underway. Have Vincent, Rey, and Nadia figure out what weapons they had, then help them try and gather them. The actions would put all the attention on them instead of luring us out, giving me some time to learn a few tricks and practice.

I hadn't the slightest idea if they were okay. Elora tried to assure us that they were fine, for now, but was vague on the details.

"They're going to use them as bait to draw everyone out." Elora explained.

"But how?" Arnessa pressed more. "You've gotten everything else right, everything down to the letter. How can we get them back without falling into their plan?"

Cat was over this deity nonsense and was sitting down now, arms wrapped around her legs. "This is going to suck hard, isn't it?"

Elora raised an eyebrow at her, but gave a single nod. "It will be difficult, yes, but if you follow along with what we've already agreed on, it'll work out just fine."

"You know Nadia doesn't work well with plans—she's not in on right? She's going to be in a throat ripping mood soon if we don't find her." I sighed, pinching the bridge of my nose as if that would compel her not to rampage against the idiots that had pulled her into this mess.

"Before we even get into that." Arnessa had been frowning for most of the conversation now. "How are they going to even use them as bait? Are they luring them into a trap or do they already have them trapped?"

Oh heck, she was right. I stared intently at Elora.

Elora paused waiting to see if anyone else had another comment. "The answer is both. She was trying to lure them into a terrible situation to make you emerge, and it failed. They are far smarter than she gave them credit for. Then, she tried to use magic against them. That also failed. Your friends quickly sorted her puzzle in record time."

Elora gave a smile before continuing, "Seeing an excellent opportunity, I finally reached out to Nadia to have them rendezvous at the mountain base. It would have worked if this Lesser Daeum wasn't so desperate. She finally captured them on their way there since the only way to stop them was for her to take direct action."

"Isn't that an illegal Daeum move?" I frowned.

"Noble Daeums follow a strict code of conduct." Elora nodded slowly. "This is a Lesser Daeum that goes by Rigyx."

"Is it just because Nobles are the good guys? Do all Lessers just lack a moral code?" I frowned, still not getting the real difference.

"Do you seek justice?" Elora asked instead.

"Yeah? I guess?" What kind of question was that? Wanting wrongs righted was a pretty normal feeling. Of course how you resolved them could be vastly different but that wasn't actually her question.

"And you've never desired to urge your magic to work just for a little fun, just to cause a little mayhem?" Elora continued her questions.

"And that's all the difference? Not falling into 'I do what I want' sort of morals?" I should have seen that coming. Lame, but not all aspects of magic fell into a gray scale, some were actually just that black and white.

"It is. You know the feel of it. It's wonderfully intoxicating. Everyone starts the same, it's how one reacts to developing their skill that determines exactly where they fall." Elora replied as if everything was that simple.

Ah, that made sense. That was why Arryn wouldn't give me an exact answer. He could help teach me, but as things progressed it would be easier to shut a Lesser

Daeum down right away instead of letting them get stronger. Elora cleared her throat, snapping my attention back to her. "Now, shall we get back to the plan?"

Arnessa let out a breath. "I think we know it. Let's just try and get this plan underway without completely messing it up."

"I'll be surprised if we don't. That's all our party is known for." Cat gave a tired smile.

I laughed at the D&D reference. Our party was often more flop and folly than suave adventurers. "I guess we start. I believe in us"

Elora nodded. "Then off you go. I'll be close behind." She vanished, all traces of her magic going with her. I wondered how she did that. I'd need to learn that little trick when this was done.

Arnessa and Cat stared at me expectantly. "Right. Guess I'm up. So, I just move us to that mountain cave."

"Should be similar to moving us to find Arryn." Arnessa smiled, trying to be encouraging.

"But with Arryn there was a magical signature." I sighed, trying to think of what exactly I could lock on to. "I don't even know where we currently are."

Cat looked thoughtful, "Well, you're technically all powerful, and just not tapped into your gifts. There should be a way to find old magical energies. Maybe just trace your own path back to that point?"

"That's brilliant." Arnessa nodded approvingly.

I had to agree. "Why are you the expert on my weird magic?" It was a rather amusing fact.

"I think the reading contest Rey and I have going has helped. We keep trying to find the strangest books with the most unique magical systems. I've won the last few months." Cat smirked. I loved how deep their geekdom went.

"I'll take it." I motioned for them to come closer as I closed my eyes.

It was easy enough to feel for my own magic. Following the trail I noticed that while others around me seemed to go cold, mine was ever vibrant. It was strong, and I felt like I could manipulate it still, despite not actually being in that past moment any longer.

That was a broken magical move. No wonder Daeums were so strong. They could likely alter things right up until a moment collided with another too powerful being. It would make Daeum dodging Daeum easier, but in the end, you could only avoid one another for so long. I wondered whose magical line was crossing whose wrongly. Rigyx's, Elora's, or maybe even mine. I was hardly sure I counted with my hardly developed magic, considering I was still figuring out how to work things. Magic didn't always care about what you felt limitations should be.

Pushing my thoughts aside, I picked up my trail once more and found the location I wanted. I dropped the magical line, not wanting to learn if I could drag us into the past, and pulled us back to the spot where we first left the caves. The magic buzzed around me rapidly and I let out a small breath, surprised by the feeling, but not feeling any negative impact.

"Sweet, you did it!" Cat cheered as she looked around.

"But goodness does everything feel wrong." Arnessa frowned, as she looked around, letting her magic seek out and find where everything was. "The magic here is different. The illusions are all wrong."

Cat frowned as well. "I sense what you're saying."

I did too. My frown echoed theirs and we all stood there, debating what exactly to do next. There was an obvious trail. We could follow it without much problems, until... "I hate them." was all that came out.

"What's wrong?" Cat asked, visibly confused by my small outburst.

My hands balled into fits. "I swear I will punch this being in the face the first chance I get."

"What is it? The trail is right here?" Arnessa was equally confused.

"The trail starts simple and branches off. Into three branches of course." I grumbled.

"Oh, they want us to split up right away." Arnessa nodded. "Smart. It'll be easy to take us down individually." The obvious trap wasn't hard to call out.

Cat shifted on her feet. "And it's easier to say you'll stick together until you get to that point. We'd have to pick who's basically more important to rescue first."

I shook my head as I thought. "No one is more important to the others. Tactically, it'll be better to rescue Vincent first. His magic would be the biggest help. Then Rey, with his healing. We'll likely need that for Nadia. She is going to shank someone the second she's freed."

"Are you okay with that plan?" Arnessa asked carefully.

"No, but it's the best plan I can come up with and Nadia would be more disappointed I didn't make a good tactical choice." I sighed. "She'd pick what's the overall best plan if she knew I was more or less all right."

"Can we cheat?" Cat asked carefully.

"What do you mean by cheat?" I raised an eyebrow at her.

"Let's just warp in there and grab Vincent, and then Rey. Walking will be exhausting, and they'll probably have traps for us along the way. If we just skip the path and get to the end goal, justice can be served more immediately." Cat replied, the idea sparking all our interest.

Arnessa nodded. "I like that idea, but what are we going to do with these idiots who are in on this dirty scheme once we reach them?"

I wasn't sure. The Stepmomster, Diamond, Melanie, and Donny were willing to work with what was essentially evil magic to further their own life plans and hurt others. My chest burned with fury, something calling from my very core that they needed to be dealt with. It would be so easy to wring their necks, or worse, but blind rage wasn't justice.

"We'll lock them up and determine their fates from there." I replied with a more simple answer than I wanted to. There were so many things that came to mind to make them pay, but true justice wasn't in their suffering. "I wonder if the unicorns would mind watching them for us."

"They wouldn't be happy about it, and erase their memories at that." Arnessa frowned.

"Exactly." Cat smirked. "Any memory of meeting the unicorns is forgotten. The perfect punishment that's not actually hurtful, and won't have any long term pain or repercussions. A more fitting fate can be determined later."

"Oh!" Arnessa's eyes sparkled with a new idea. "I don't know if that idea is even cheating. It fits more with cheesing, as you said." Arnessa mused, pausing for effect, as she flashed Cat a smile. "Cheating would be locating our group and bringing them here."

"Daeums are that overpowered, aren't they?" I gave a small laugh. "I'm not sure if I can do all that, but getting to their location shouldn't be a problem. I can follow their paths easily enough."

"Can you try bringing them here?" Arnessa asked curiously. "It would save us a lot of grief."

I considered what she said for a moment. Could I? It should be as easy as following their paths and just bringing them here instead of us to them. Maybe even easier than moving us. I wasn't sure. I reached out and tried to locate them all together but it was too difficult to sense them all at once. It didn't feel impossible, but my skill was nowhere near that level.

"I'll have to do this one at a time, but it'll be worth trying." I finally agreed.

Closing my eyes, I started with Vincent. He was unconscious, but seemed otherwise fine. I could feel the magic of two others with him, but it was simple enough to ignore them and leave them alone there. It was easy to wrap my magic around just Vincent, and ta-da! I felt his presence by my side as I pulled him magically to me. Arnessa audibly gasped as she rushed to him, but I ignored them, keeping my eyes closed as I moved my focus to Rey.

He seemed to be in slightly better shape, no surprise with his strong magic. Rey was a fast healer because of it, so I had no doubt he'd soon be fine. There was only one person guarding him, and they felt rather underpowered. Again, easy enough to ignore. With a pull, Rey was back with us. Cat's reaction was exactly the same as Arnessa's. They had both been so worried about their loves. I didn't blame them.

Time to bring my love to me. After all that had transpired in such a short time, I needed her back with me.

I followed the path, her trail easy for me to see, almost easier than the other too until it stopped. A strong force blocked it and I cursed. "They're on to me."

"What?" Arnessa asked.

I opened my eyes, not bothering to hide my rage. "She figured out what I was doing and blocked me. I don't know how to get around it."

Cat helped Rey sit up as he regained consciousness. "We'll just have to go to her and punch her in the face then."

"I do want to do that." I agreed, not feeling any bit better about the idea.

"What's going on?" Rey looked around confused before smiling at Cat. "I have no idea how you found us."

Cat smiled in return before kissing his cheek. "It's complicated, but the short is, we need to get Nadia back."

Rey groaned. "That'll be easy once I don't feel like I was thrown into a wall."

"Were you thrown into a wall?" Concern filled Cat's eyes.

"Yeah, we all were." Rey glanced my way, not wanting to meet my eyes. "Nadia was probably hit the hardest."

Fury filled me, magic sparkling along my entire being.

"Cool it, wannabe god." Arnessa called sharply.

The words threw me off for a moment, helping to take the magic down a notch. I didn't need to be a crazy deity. I hardly felt like one as it was.

Vincent gave a groan as he started to stir.

Rey made a similar sound as he moved to him, starting to heal Vincent without a second thought.

"Are you sure you're okay to do that?" Cat asked worriedly.

"I have enough extra magic to get him going." Rey grimaced but stubbornly kept healing.

"Don't overdo it. We don't have time for that." Cat warned him.

We really didn't. I was antsy, ready to continue on by myself, but I knew that was exactly what they wanted. The carrot dangled so perfectly in front of me. I'd be a fool to take it, but heavens knew it was hard not to.

Arnessa helped Vincent up as Rey healed him. Cat gave a very vague run down of what was going on. While she kept the Daeum parts a secret, she did mention some beings here had managed to help me with my magic.

"If it's enough to take them down. Let's do this." Rey said getting up and stretching.

"I'm not sure you two are well enough for this." I frowned.

Vincent waved off my concern. "It'll be fine." Arnessa helped Vincent up.

I wasn't sure I trusted that statement, but I was already having trouble not leaving the group. "I guess we're good to go then."

"Let's do it." Cat smirked motioning for me to lead on. "Where's the path?"

I set off, knowing they would all follow.

The path was easy to follow. Or at least it was clear to magically feel out. I knew exactly where I needed to go, but the forest was difficult to navigate. Fallen trees, gnarled roots, and so many wisps of negative magic making me momentarily wonder if we were being followed.

We weren't, not exactly. I was sure the Lesser Daeum, this Rigyx being, was monitoring our every move, waiting patiently, toying with us for their amusement as we followed the path.

Finally I could feel in the distance where the block was. "Strong magic ahead. It's whatever was keeping me from Nadia earlier." I informed them as we traveled.

"Awesome. Stop!" Cat called out to me .

"What? Why?" I stopped as she requested.

"Because this is where the traps gotta be." Cat pointed out the obvious.

I nodded. "Good point, but what can it be?"

"They were trying to seperate us earlier." Arnessa reminded me. "I wouldn't be surprised if you stayed ahead if you could pass this block and we couldn't."

"That would be the best bet." I agreed, feeling a small sense of defeat. "How can we get around it? I can't even tell how Nadia is anymore. We need to get to her, now."

I looked at Cat the same time as Arnessa did causing Vincent and Rey both to give us confused looks.

"Why would you know?" Rey asked Cat, voicing the confusion for the both of them.

Cat shrugged. "I've been really *really* good at guessing how Ash's power up could work."

I chuckled. "She knows more about my magic than me."

"It's been really helpful." Arnessa agreed.

"We're missing something." Vincent eyed Arnessa carefully. "What else happened?"

Arnessa fidgeted with her sleeve while Cat spoke up instead. "It's complicated, but awesome. You'll have to wait and see." She turned her attention to me. "I've got an idea."

"I'm all ears." I was really curious where she came up with all these ideas.

Cat dropped her voice so low I could barely hear her. "Can you get us all in there? I know you can't get Nadia out, but maybe it still works the other way?"

Rey shook his head. "I don't know the full scope of things, but I'm thinking that's not going to happen."

"Well, what's your idea if that's the circumstance?" Cat turned to him.

"I'm thinking we lure whoever it is out?" Rey shrugged. "It's not a video game so they aren't leashed to the area. Maybe we can lure them out. Shouldn't be hard if it's that nutball Donny."

"That's if we can get close enough for them to see us, and if it's Donny. If it's the Lesser Daeum then they'll just wait it out. They've got all the time in the world." Cat argued, easily continuing the debate.

"We can try plan A and figure out a B if it's not Donny." Rey suggested. "Or if Ash can feel where Nadia is, maybe she can tell if Donny is there too?"

They both turned toward me. I shrugged and closed my eyes, trying to get any feeling of who is in there. "He's certainly there but he feels… different. Like he's infused with magic he shouldn't have. There's another there too. I don't know them so maybe the Lesser Daeum." I opened my eyes as Cat and Rey resumed their debate.

"So it would work if it was just Donny, but he has someone to stop him from being a complete imbecile. We can't rely on anyone dispelling it either way." Cat said.

Rey shrugged. "It would help if we still had that bow that always hits its target. If we could figure out where the Lesser Daeum is, the arrow would go through the barrier."

"But she would have to be physical." Cat argued. "Daeum's can be present without being physical."

"As much as I love this debate, and I really do," Vincent interrupted, "Why don't we try dismantling the barrier?" We all gave him a surprised look. "I mean, there's five of us. At worst, combined, we should be able to at least make a hole so we can all get in and solve this."

We all stared at him, surprised that it really could be that simple. He didn't even know exactly what my extra power was yet. Maybe we really could do this. We could save Nadia, and flush this Lesser Daeum out of hiding.

"Let's do it then. I'm sure together we can make a hole or break it down." I readily agreed, setting off once more.

Cat and Arnessa sped up to walk just a step in front of me. The gesture mildly amused me. I could tell they were concerned, and they were right to be. I was too over being torn away from my life and my love. This needed to end. Now.

We quickly reached the barrier. It was hard to see but oh so easy to feel with it magic sending tingly vibes of dread our way.

"Is it supposed to make us leery?" Rey laughed. "What a great way to try and trick us into walking through it."

Cat snorted but didn't comment.

"Alright, does anyone actually know how to take down this kind of magic?" Vincent asked, staying on point.

I nodded. "I have before when I first met Nadia. It was a lot more low key than this though."

"But you can point our magic in the right direction can't you?" Rey asked curiously.

"I think so." I hesitantly agreed.

"Let's do this then." Vincent shot me a smile.

Arnessa and Cat interlaced their hands in mine before grabbing the guys' hands on either side of them. I closed my eyes and concentrated on the magic, looking for that Daeum hum.

It sounded like a high school band's experimental music. Everything was off, screechy, and made me cringe. It certainly followed the same pattern but goodness! did I hate everything about it. If the Lesser Daeums weren't notably evil, this alone could drive the Noble ones mad. Did that include me? It was maddening, but I wasn't sure I was ready to think of myself in that way. Not yet anyway.

When the predictable pattern was easy to see, I tugged at everyone's magic, pulling it with mine to dismantle the threads. I could feel the barrier breaking down and magically tugged us all inside, warping us the few needed feet before the Lesser Daeum could restring the threads.

I opened my eyes, letting my friends' magic go as instant rage filled me. There was Nadia, roped several different ways to a tree with Donny at her side. He looked surprised to see us, a whip in his hand raised high, ready to strike. Blood already coated Nadia's side.

A smile crossed Donny's face, slowly. The motion looked crazed, as if he had wanted nothing more than to see us. Than to see me.

The whip fell from his hand. "Ah, there's my beautiful Belle," he said with arms open wide before laughing as he shook his head. "Too bad I didn't want these guests."

With a snap of his fingers, vines shot up from the ground, ensnaring and pulling them all down except me.

Magic radiated off me, coming in furious waves. "You will either let them go now, or find you have no magic left in your entire being." I said through gritted teeth, trying hard not to obliterate him where he stood.

Donny laughed. The idiot just laughed and laughed, carefree as if he didn't see, as if he didn't feel the layers of magic pulsing off of me. "My dearest Belle, I am far stronger than you think now. You are mine, and you will *never* be able to leave me."

Vines shot up around me, snaking around my legs and torso before taking hold of my arms. Thorns pricked me, digging in where the vines wrapped too tightly in certain places. Some enough to draw blood. He gave a laugh as if that was the end of everything.

The vines meant nothing to me. "This is your final warning."

Donny chuckled darkly as he casually strolled up to me. "My darling, I think you're very mistaken." He reached out to caress my cheek.

The second his skin came into contact with mine, it burned his hand, causing him to jump back and scream as intense pain wracked his nerves, leaving a burn that made a blazing fire look friendly.

"You're out of warnings." I snarled as the vines around me disintegrated.

I let my magic pulse out, seeking and destroying the vines and freeing my friends. I could hear their relief as I approached Donny, who was still shaking out his hand, as if that would make the pain stop.

"You were told to leave me alone but you just couldn't do that, now, could you?" I grabbed a hold of his good arm, causing him to freeze in place. There were so many ways I wanted, no needed, to make him pay.

But I held back. "Good night, Donny." I said to him, putting him in a deep trance, willing it so that the only one who could wake him was me.

My magic wasn't finished and I could feel that Lesser Daeum watching us, their magic just out of reach... Or was it?

I pulled on the feeling of it with everything I had. All the fury and rage I felt making it easy to grab onto her own chaotic magic. Suddenly she was right in front of me.

Her lips were all that was visible, the surprise quickly wiping away as she gave a small sultry smile. "So, you finally figured out how to find me and join our kind?"

I narrowed my eyes at her. "My kind is nothing like you." I reached out to grab hold of her but she stepped back, cackling madly.

"You think someone like you can take me down so easily?" Her voice was light and airy, as if she had expected this all along.

"No, I know I can." I smirked, the perfect opportunity arising.

I moved to grab her again, and to no surprise she moved back, just as fast as before. Only she didn't notice the truest master of illusion and stealth behind her. Arryn closed the gap, ramming his horn into her.

The Lesser Daeum gasped, a mixture of surprise and pain covering her face as Elora appeared. "Hello Rigyx. Long time no see."

The Lesser Daeum looked genuinely terrified to see the Noble Daeum.

"What? Unicorn got your tongue?" Elora cackled in a way that was so dark I took a step back. "I think it's time we took this meeting elsewhere." She looked at me with a sweet smile. "I'll be in touch. Until then, return home. You'll see her magic is out of your life now."

Elora and Arryn vanished with the Lesser Daeum.

Relief only lasted for a moment before I rushed to free Nadia. Her magic felt tight and frayed, and I hoped willing mine to soothe her would be enough to heal her and help her return to her true form.

Within a few moments she was human again. Bloody and tired, but human. I held her close to my chest as the others approached.

"What just happened?" Vincent looked horrified as Rey came to check on Nadia.

"It's a long story. Let's get home first, then we'll explain." I promised. "Someone pull the blockhead closer. I'm not sure I can do that much more ranged magic." Exhaustion filled every little nook and crevice, but I was determined to get us out of here.

Once everyone was close together again, I easily found home. It was the clearest song to my heart, and to my joy and relief, took no effort to bring us back.

Home at last.

EPILOGUE

----Elora----

New Daeums were always tricky to teach. Not because it was hard, but because it was almost impossible to tell how they would react to their gifts. Astrid had zero desire to consider herself what she was. A Daeum.

While she loved the magic, and loved even more learning every last aspect of it, there was no convincing her of her new title. It didn't matter much, there was no changing that fact even if she didn't want to accept it. Astrid was very well committed to taking the Noble route, and that was all that mattered in the end.

With new magic learned and under her belt, it was finally time to show her the dark side of things. Sometimes even a Noble Daeum needed to do vile magic to keep the universe safe.

"I'm ready." she said neutrally as we descended the dungeon stairs where Donny was being held.

Mages didn't realize that while yes, a being could be stripped of their magic, it still needed to go somewhere. "Good. You know what to do then."

We walked to his cell, Nadia just a step behind us. "It's finally ending." She breathed a sigh of relief.

Ash glanced back at her with a sad smile. "It is. I had really hoped it wouldn't come to this but after that last adventure…" Her voice trailed off.

Nothing more needed to be said. The man was psychotic at best, and after being tainted with such vile magic he would never be the same again anyway.

As we reached the cell, Donny was lying on the floor, staring off into nothing as he muttered to himself. The words came out a jumbled mess, not a single sentence able to be formed.

"The others are lucky they only have life in prison." Nadia clicked her tongue as we watched Donny for a moment. "This is not a good way to go."

"He's already gone." Ash shrugged. "Now justice will be served."

Magic radiated around her. It felt too warm for comfort, edging on hot. With a snap of her hands Donny sat up for a moment before collapsing to the floor once more. All the magic pulled from his being in one simple motion.

Ash closed her eyes as she let out a steady breath. "There, I think it's done."

I concentrated for a brief moment, feeling Donnys magic going from human back into the universe's ebb and flow where it needed to be. "Perfect."

Ash smiled and turned to Nadia. "Good. I've got a happily ever after to get back to."

I chuckled but didn't comment on it. "Until we meet again." I gave them a small bow knowing we'd meet on much better terms in the future.

We were the magic that made fantasy turn into fairytale, that brought everything in the universe back to where it needed to be. Happily ever after was exactly where our magic would always lead.

BONUS SCENE

Bonus Scene

----Rose----

The rain bounced gleefully off my umbrella as I walked into Snakes. That wasn't exactly the name of the place, but the prison looked like a snake the way the buildings weaved around so, who cared? The name didn't matter. The only thing that was important was the envelope in my hands.

Security was a breeze. I had nothing to hide, and greatly enjoyed showing and discussing the contents of what I brought. The guards got a laugh out of everything and after a while of talking, ushered me through.

The walls here were boring, offwhite, and relatively free of anything. A few signs pointed where to go, what to do, but nothing more. After two more gates, I reached a sitting room.

The walls here were an odd shade of green. As if they were painted decades ago and never redone. The faded colors felt wrong. I could take darkness. I could take brightness. I loathed poorly kept up places. Thankfully, I wouldn't be here long.

Finally, a guard ushered in a handcuffed Diamond and Mother. Bracelets around their wrists and ankles glowed a soft silver. The devices would likely never be allowed off, forever keeping their magic at bay. They were lucky to have their minds still. That creep-in-a-box Donny didn't anymore.

The thought caused a smile to spread across my face. Something about him was vile, more so than Mother.

"What do you want?" my birthgiver asked as she was forced into the chair across from me. While it was cushioned, it looked about as old as the room did.

"I thought you would love to see these." I replied calmly, holding up an envelope.

I didn't offer it to her. Instead I opened it and pulled out the first picture. Diamond rolled her eyes, sitting with arms crossed from her seat.

"We don't want to see those, traitor."

I ignored my sister and happily explained it. "I was one of the major supporting roles in our last production. My mentor believes I have a great shot at the lead in our next show."

I went through picture after picture of the latest ballet production I was in. Neither woman in front of me cared. I wasn't expecting them to. Even freed they only would have attended to try and schmooze with the bigger names in attendance.

"What are you doing here?" Mother asked firmly as I finally finished my small show of pictures.

"I wanted to thank you actually." I grinned, having planned and worked through what I was going to say for several days now.

"Doubtful." Di grumbled.

"Oh, but I do." My smile widened. "Like, at first I was devastated. My fam was gone. But you know, I totes realized it wasn't. I was only the pretty little thing that got you some attention in our small town. You out of the picture has been amazeballs. I see that now. There is zero difference. Nothing has changed."

"You should watch your manners. I am your mother!" my birthgiver shrieked at me.

It was expected though. Her change in volume and tone did nothing to me. "You're right. One thing did change. My stepsister actually likes my shows." I pulled out the last picture I had been saving. Arnessa and I side by side, the bouquet of stunning flowers she brought in my hands. I don't remember any other photo I had smiled as happily in.

I put the photos away as I headed out, the guards restraining my disowned family members as they screamed at me, screamed about her putting them in here. The exact words didn't reach me. I had my closure, and was grateful to have honest support for the first time in my life.

CHARACTER PROFILES

Arnessa:
Full Name: Arnessa Lilith Frell
Birthday: May 18th
Magic: Illusions, Potions, Conjuration
Eye color: Carmel
Hair color: Black
Bisexual
First Appearance: An Unexpected Brew

Vincent:
Full Name: Alexander Vincent Reming
Birthday: September 26th
Magic: Illusions, Destruction, Enchanting
Eye color: Blue
Hair color: Dark Brown
Metrosexual
First Appearance: An Unexpected Brew

Rey:
Full Name: Reyfair Sebastian Mountbatten
Birthday: March 25th
Magic: Healing, Animal Speak, Wards
Eye color: Dark Brown
Hair color: Brown
Demiromatic Bisexual

First Appearance: For The Guild

Cat:
Full Name: Catara Nicole Crosswhite
Birthday: October 29th
Magic: Enchanting, Stoneflesh, Telekinesis (minor)
Eye color: Gray Blue
Hair color: Blonde
Demisexual
First Appearance: For The Guild

Ash:
Full Name: Astrid Thŭmby Seth
Birthday: January 3rd
Magic: Raw Magic, Hear Animals
Eye color: Brown
Hair color: Dark Brown
Gray Romantic
First Appearance: Of Beasts And Bells

Nadia:
Full Name: Nadia Liang Yuan
Birthday: December 6th
Magic: Dire Red Wolf form, Otter Form, Mental Communication
Eye color: Hazel
Hair color: Black

Pansexual
First Appearance: Of Beasts And Bells

Secondary Characters:

Diamond:
Full Name: Diamond Annmarie Tremaine
Birthday: July 3rd
Magic: Potions (very minor)
Eye Color: Amber
Hair Color: Rose Gold (dyed)
Arnessa's step-sister
Straight
First Appearance: An Unexpected Brew

Rose:
Full Name: Rose Alyshia Tremaine
Birthday: March 24th
Magic: Gravity Manipulation (very minor)
Eye Color: Amber
Hair Color: Rose Gold (dyed)
Arnessas's step-sister
Bisexual
First Appearance: An Unexpected Brew

Henrietta:
Full Name: Henrietta Louise Tremaine
Birthday: December 16th
Magic: Void (minor)
Eye Color: Amber
Hair Color: Dark
Arnessa's step-mother
Unknown Orientation
First Appearance: An Unexpected Brew

Melanie:
Full Name: Melanie Renee Crosswhite
Birthday: April 7th
Magic: Ice
Eye Color: Green
Hair Color: Dark Blonde
Cat's half-sister
Pansexual
First Appearance: For The Guild

Donny:
Full Name: Donny Ross LeGume
Birthday: June 18th
Magic: Tracking
Eye Color: Brown
Hair Color: Black
Straight

First Appearance: Of Beasts And Bells

Marcus:
Full Name: Marcus Rajesh Seth
Birthday: November 19th
Magic: Computer
Eye Color: Brown
Hair Color: Dark Brown
Ash's Brother
Ace
First Appearance: Of Beasts And Bells

TIMELINE

Kyklos year 1323
-Summer: Ash and Nadia Meet
-Fall school semester: Rey and Cat meet
-Halfway into fall semester: Arnessa and Vincent meet

Kyklos 1324
-Spring: Arnessa and Vincent get engaged
-Summer: everyone meets at an event, group shortly starts online meetups and D&D sessions
-Fall: first in-person D&D meetup.

Kyklos 1325
Winter: January Cat and Rey get engaged, Arnessa and Vincent announce the wedding for early fall.
Summer: this story occurs at the end of September.

ACKNOWLEDGMENTS

Aud: I really could not have done this without you. Thank you for pointing out all the little things that needed to be fixed with so many interweaving perspectives.

Geetha: thank you for asking about the stepevils. You inspired that bonus scene. It was fun seeing exactly where Rose could go with a little less negative influence.

Elyse: I love you sis. Thank you for your continued support and may your happily ever afters continue to be abundant.

To my niblings: you are all too small to read this yet, but I look forward to leaving you books to grow into. I love you, all the lots.

As always, to my cats. You're adorable but the djkfn%lsg5nslui_rgas needed to be removed. It's the thought that counts.

ABOUT THE AUTHOR

Mueller is a midwesterner who was born and raised in IL where she currently resides. While unicorns and magic sparked an interest in the genre, it was childhood friends that convinced her to write, and turn to a life of whimsy. Mueller has been described as two penguins in a trench coat though nothing has been proven just yet. Currently, Mueller is focused on writing all things magical and adores having characters battle curses, tangle with spirits, and face off against wicked family members for a chance at a better ending.

Facebook Group:

GoodReads: https://www.goodreads.com/author/show/16958250.J_E_Mueller

Bookbub: https://www.bookbub.com/profile/j-e-mueller

ALSO BY J.E. MUELLER

To find more of Mueller's work please visit Amazon or Goodreads.

A Tune of Demons

-Fire's Song

-Spirit's Lullaby

-Dream's Melody

Once Upon An Adventure

-An Unexpected Brew

-For The Guild

-Of Beasts And Bells

-Once Upon An Adventure

By The Skies